"How long have you known exactly who I am?"

"As soon as I learned your name. Why wouldn't I realize that you're the CEO of Aldrich Supermarkets?"

Tyler sighed. With stores across the state of Oklahoma, had he really thought she wouldn't know?

"I won't tell anyone, if it's that important to you," Charlottte vowed softly.

He nodded. "Yeah, okay. Thanks." Then a horrible thought occurred to him. "*That's* why they were all so friendly to me today. The whole town must know!"

"Now, that's just silly," Charlotte told him. "Folks in Eden are naturally friendly. It has nothing to do with who your family is!"

"How do I know that?"

"Oh, Tyler, not everyone is after your money."

He wanted to flee—except that he didn't really have anyplace to go or anything to do. And he didn't want to be alone.

For once, Tyler realized, he really wanted not to be alone.

Books by Arlene James

Love Inspired

*Everyday Miracles
**Eden, OK

ARLENE JAMES

says, "Camp meetings, mission work and the church where my parents and grandparents were prominent members permeate my Oklahoma childhood memories. It was a golden time, which sustains me yet. However, only as a young, widowed mother did I truly begin growing in my personal relationship with the Lord. Through adversity, He blessed me in countless ways, one of which is a second marriage so loving and romantic it still feels like courtship!"

The author of more than sixty novels, Arlene James now resides outside of Dallas, Texas, with her husband. Arlene says, "The rewards of motherhood have indeed been extraordinary for me. Yet I've looked forward to this new stage of my life." Her need to write is greater than ever, a fact that frankly amazes her, as she's been at it since the eighth grade!

His Small-Town Girl
Arlene James

Steeple
Hill®

Published by Steeple Hill Books™

STEEPLE HILL BOOKS

Steeple Hill®

ISBN-13: 978-0-373-81363-6
ISBN-10:   0-373-81363-5

HIS SMALL-TOWN GIRL

www.SteepleHill.com

Printed in U.S.A.

Then the King will say to those on His right,
Come, you who are blessed of my Father, inherit
the kingdom prepared for you from the foundation
of the world. For I was hungry, and you gave me
something to eat; I was thirsty, and you gave me
drink; I was a stranger, and you invited me in.

—*Matthew* 25:34-35

To Virginia, because friends are just chosen family, because sisterhood in Christ runs deeper than blood, because there's always lots of living left to be done and because it's never too late to find love.

Chapter One

The sweet, clean aroma of freshly harvested fields invaded the low-slung sports car as it flew along the narrow ribbon of road, its sun roof open to the autumn breeze. Tyler sucked in a deep breath, feeling the last of his tension drain away, as if a great weight had lifted from his chest. Finally.

When he'd walked out of the board meeting in Dallas, almost four hours ago now on this last day in a long and difficult week, his only thought had been to find some peace somewhere. For Tyler this meant shutting off his cell phone, climbing into his expensive cinnamon-red car and hitting the road for a good, long drive. Operating from sheer impulse, he'd headed north, avoiding the most well-traveled roads, and now he found himself in Oklahoma on Highway 81, a smooth, level two-lane stretch with little traffic for a Friday afternoon.

A blinking yellow light brought his attention to

the dashboard. He depressed a button on the steering column and saw via a digital readout that at his current rate of speed he could drive exactly 8.9 miles with the fuel remaining in his gas tank. Time to pull over. A glance at the in-dash clock showed him that the hour had gone six already.

Glancing around in the dusky light of an autumn evening beginning to fade into night, he saw nothing but empty fields bisected with the occasional lazily drifting line of trees and railroad tracks running at twenty or thirty yards distant alongside the highway. Bowie, the last town he'd passed before crossing the Red River, lay many miles behind him to the south, many more than he could cover with the fuel remaining in the tank, anyway. There must be a local source of gasoline, however. People had to drive around here, didn't they? Wherever here was.

Tapping the screen of his in-dash global positioning system, Tyler noted that the small community of Eden, Oklahoma, some 2.3 miles ahead, offered a gasoline station. Confident that he would find what he needed there, he sped off.

Moments later, a female voice announced, "Right turn ahead." Seconds after that, the GPS intoned, "Right turn in two miles." Less than a minute later that changed to, "After two hundred yards, turn right. Then turn left."

Braking, he reached over and shut off the voice prompt. "Thank you, darlin'. I'll take it from here."

When he turned off the highway onto the broad, dusty street, given the appearance of the few buildings he passed, the whole place seemed deserted, and the quaint three-pump filling station that he pulled into some moments later proved no exception. The overhanging shadow of an immense tree all but obscured the faded sign that identified the station as Froggy's Gas And Tire.

Engine throbbing throatily, Tyler eased the sleek auto close enough to the door to read the posted business hours, which were 6:00 a.m. to 6:00 p.m., Monday through Saturday. Used to twenty-four-hour service, Tyler felt his jaw drop. Six to six? And closed on Sundays? Talk about turning back time.

Shaking his head, he tapped the GPS again and learned, to his chagrin, that the next nearest station could be found in Waurika, some 19 miles distant. A check on his fuel status showed a mere 6.1 miles left in his tank, thanks to his burst of speed back there, which meant... The implications hit him like a ton of bricks.

Stuck! He was stuck in the middle of nowhere. At least until six o'clock in the morning.

His intent had been to get away from the fighting, arguments and manipulation for a while, not to disappear for a whole night. He hadn't brought so much as a toothbrush with him, let alone a change of clothing. Clearly, he had to do something.

Finding solutions had become his stock-in-trade. In fact, that very trait had prompted his father to choose him over his older sister and younger brother to head the family company, much to the angry disappointment of his siblings.

Tyler reached for his cell phone. As with most businessmen, the mobile phone constituted both a necessity and an irritant for Tyler Aldrich. In the ten months since he'd been named CEO of the Aldrich & Associates Grocery store chain, it had become more headache than help, giving his family unfettered access to his ear, into which they never missed an opportunity to pour complaints, arguments and increasingly shrill demands. No doubt by now they'd filled his mailbox with as many acrimonious messages as it would hold. Nevertheless, the phone was his ticket out of here. He'd simply call for assistance—or would have if he'd had service.

Tyler sat for several moments staring at the tiny screen in his hand, disbelief rounding his light blue eyes. He'd switch to a satellite phone the instant he got back to Texas!

Even as he wondered how the people around here got along without cell-phone service, the thought of satellites calmed him. The phone might not work, but the car's satellite uplink obviously did or he'd have no GPS. Duh. He hit the button on the dashboard and put his head back, waiting for the connection to be made and an operator's voice to offer help through a tiny speaker just above the driver's door.

After Tyler identified himself and stated his

problem, the customer service rep assured him that help would reach him in four to six hours. Dumbfounded, Tyler began to shake his head, wondering how he might pass the time.

He looked around him. A sheet-metal fence enclosed what appeared to be a scrap yard, flanked on one side by the filling station and on the other by a small, shingled house with a tall, concrete stoop. The house stood as dark and silent as the station. Otherwise, Tyler would have been tempted to knock on the door in hopes of rousting the station's proprietor.

With no immediate options presenting themselves, he checked out the local accommodations via the GPS. He found just two listings, a café and the Heavenly Arms Motel.

He'd passed the motel on his way into town. Not at all up to his usual standards, it had appeared neat and clean, at least, but he could not quite resign himself to spending the night away from home when a tank of gas would have him on his doorstep before—he checked his watch—3:00 a.m. If he was lucky. Better check out that café and tank up on coffee.

A short drive around town revealed a liberal sprinkling of oil pumps across the landscape. One even occupied a bare patch of dirt next to the tiny city hall, a modern contrast to the three blocks of storefronts that seemed to comprise "downtown" Eden. Most looked as if they'd been built in the

1930s. And every one sat locked up tight as a drum, including the Garden of Eden café.

In fact, except for the old-fashioned streetlights and a few silently glowing windows of the modest homes lining the broad streets, Eden, Oklahoma, might have been a ghost town. That evoked an odd sense of loneliness in Tyler, as if everyone had a place to go except him. Well, he'd wanted peace and quiet; could be, he'd gotten more than he'd bargained for.

Easing the expensive sports car back out onto 81, he noted wryly a small sign that proclaimed, You're In Eden, God's Country And The Land Of Oil!

God apparently closed up shop at 6:00 p.m. sharp. Someone, thankfully, had forgotten to tell the local motel, though.

The low, lit sign that stood in a narrow patch of grass in front of the small motel glowed invitingly in the deepening gloom. The Heavenly Arms Motel, it read, Low Rates, Monthly, Weekly, Nightly. Family Owned And Operated.

Surely he could spend a few hours there. At the very least, he ought to find some information and possibly even assistance. All he needed were a few gallons of high-test, after all. Failing that, he could always get a room. He made a left just past the sign and pulled up beneath the overhang at the end of the main building, which looked more like a stylized ranch house than a motel lobby. A sign on the edge of the overhang proclaimed, Vacancy, which did not surprise him one bit.

Tyler killed the engine and got out of the car. The air held a crispness that he had not yet noticed in a Dallas October, which accounted for his lack of an overcoat. Bypassing a small side window to be used, according to the accompanying sign, after 10:00 p.m., Tyler followed a concrete ramp to the narrow porch that ran the length of the front of the building.

He opened the door marked Welcome and walked into a homey room complete with a polished wood floor, worn leather couches and, in the very center of the room, a six-sided game table surrounded by an equal number of chairs. A potbellied stove squatted in one corner. In another stood a chest-high, L-shaped counter with a pair of black painted doors behind it.

The far door bore a sign proclaiming it the office. The other door was marked Private. Through that door a young woman appeared mere seconds later, smiling as if greeting a lifelong friend.

"Hello. How are you?"

A pretty little thing with thick, light auburn hair that fell from a slight widow's peak in a long braid down the center of her back, she stood no more than average height, the comfortable jeans and faded chambray shirt beneath her white bibbed apron somehow emphasizing her slight frame, just as the widow's peak emphasized the shape of her face, a slender, slightly elongated heart.

Despite delicate features and a smattering of freckles across the nose, her finest assets were large, hazel eyes—a vivid amalgam of gold, silvery-blue and muted green—thickly fringed with platinum and framed by slender brows. She wore no cosmetics and no visible jewelry, but then she didn't need to. Such beauty required no accessory beyond wholesomeness, and that she possessed in abundance.

Tyler might have brusquely stated his problem, could even have complained. Instead, he found himself returning her smile, a sense of delight eclipsing his irritation. Natural, well-used charm effortlessly oozed forth.

"Since you asked," he replied lightly in answer to her question, "I'm stranded. Yourself?"

Her smiled widened, and his spirits unaccountably lifted.

"Never better, thank you."

She untied the strings around her slender waist and lifted the apron off over her head before neatening the rolled cuffs of her long sleeves. Her thick braid swung over one shoulder, and her waist nipped in neatly where her shirt tucked into the band of her jeans. Tyler abruptly found himself thinking that he might as well spend the night.

For once he didn't have a Friday-evening engagement. Maybe, he thought, he'd even forget tomorrow's plans and stay the whole weekend. Why not? Might do his contentious family some good to wonder where he'd gotten to.

His mother didn't need an audience in order to complain about his late father's grasping second wife, anyway, and his sister and brother would just have to argue between themselves. He didn't give a second thought to the luxury stadium box where he routinely hosted guests less interested in professional football than in being seen with the right people, none of whom would ever think to look for him here.

For the first time in memory, he could simply let down his guard and be. It almost seemed foreign, such relaxation. Yet he shoved aside the niggling thoughts of responsibility, albeit responsibilities he'd strived to earn and fought to keep. Sometimes, responsibility just seemed to weigh too much. He deserved a little break, and Eden, it suddenly seemed, really did exist.

At least for the moment.

Charlotte recognized money when she saw it, especially when it stood right in front of her. One got used to all sorts in this business, from the most hopeless and downtrodden of God's children to the most flagrantly unlovable, and in her experience, those with the most money often fell into the latter category. They came in demanding more than they surely knew they could expect and often went away angry and dissatisfied, in spite of her best efforts to provide what they needed. That possibility was not what disturbed her about this particular gentleman, however.

For some reason, with barely a flick of his pale blue gaze, he made her nervous, self-conscious in ways she hadn't felt in years. Tall and fit with stunning pale blue eyes and thick, dark hair that swept back from his square-jawed face in subdued waves, he differed significantly from their normal clientele.

For one thing, she'd rarely—okay, never—seen such a well-dressed, well-groomed gentleman. Oh, more than one well-heeled type had wandered in after finding themselves stranded, usually in the middle of the night, but something told her that even those folks operated in a social strata below this particular guest.

Other than that, though, she couldn't really put her finger on what made him so different. She only knew that he undoubtedly was, which did not mean that she would treat him any differently than she treated anyone else. Just the opposite, in fact. Her Christian principles demanded nothing less.

She ratcheted her smile up another notch and asked, "How can I help you?"

He sighed, making a rueful sound. "Unless you've got a few spare gallons of gasoline around, I guess I'll be needing a room for the night."

No surprise there. She'd heard this story before. Obviously, he should've kept a closer eye on the gas gauge. Giving her head a shake, she jerked a thumb over one shoulder.

"Sorry. That old truck out back runs on diesel.

The room I can manage, though, if you can do without a kitchenette." She plunked down a registration form and pen, explaining, "Our regulars prefer them, so they're almost always taken."

"Regulars?" He sounded surprised, even skeptical.

"Most are oil-field workers who come to town periodically to service the local lines and pumps."

"You've got plenty of those around," he murmured, scribbling his information on the form.

"We sure do," she replied, taking a key from the rack hidden beneath the counter. "You're in—"

"Oil country," he finished for her, glancing up with a smile. "Or is that God's country?"

"Both," she confirmed with a smile, "but I was going to say number eight. Back row, south end. That's to your right. Your covered parking will be to the left of your door."

"Covered parking," he mused, clearly pleased by that.

"That'll be forty dollars and sixty-six cents, including tax."

Pulling his wallet from the inside pocket of his expertly tailored suit coat, he thumbed through the bills until he found a fifty-dollar bill. She unlocked her cash drawer and counted out his change while glancing over his registration form. When she got to the part concerning the make and model of his car, she understood why that covered parking had made such an impression.

Little garages, really, but without doors, the spaces were open only on one end. Her grandfather took inordinate pride in providing them for their guests, but none of them, Charlotte felt sure, had ever offered protection to anything remotely comparable to the car of—she peeked at his registration again—Tyler Aldrich. Well, no wonder. She casually shifted her gaze to the side window.

So that's what a hundred-thousand bucks on wheels looked like. Smiling, she shoved a bunch of bills and coins at him, as if he needed nine dollars and thirty-four cents in change.

No doubt the rooms he usually rented cost ten times as much as what she had to offer. Then again, he happened to need what she had to offer.

Maybe he could afford a hundred-thousand-dollar car, but, as her grandfather Hap would say, he put his pants on just like everyone else; therefore, she would treat him like everyone else. She put out her hand.

"I'm Charlotte Jefford. Welcome to Eden, Mr. Aldrich."

"Thanks." Sliding his long, square palm against hers, he asked smoothly, "Is that Mrs. Jefford?"

Charlotte paused. Curiosity, she wondered, or flirtation? The next moment she realized that it couldn't possibly be the latter, and even if it was, it simply didn't matter. "Miss."

He smiled and let go of her hand. "Miss Jefford, then, could you advise me where I might find a meal? One that someone else prepares, that is, since the kitchenette is out of the question."

Charlotte laughed. "Easily. After dusk there's just the Watermelon Patch, about a half mile north of town. Can't miss it. Best fried catfish in the county."

He made a face. "Any chance they serve anything that's not fried?"

She considered a moment. "Beans and cole slaw." This did not seem to excite him. "They do baked potatoes on Saturday nights."

"That's a big help," he pointed out wryly, "since this is Friday."

"The truck stop in Waurika doesn't close until ten," she offered guiltily, thinking of the meat loaf she'd just pulled from the oven. "You can get a salad there." Provided he considered iceberg lettuce and a sprinkling of shredded carrots a salad.

"If I could get to Waurika, I wouldn't need a room," he pointed out with a sigh.

"Oh. Right." She bit her lip, glanced again out the window at that sleek red fortune-on-wheels and knew that her hesitation did not become her. If he'd pulled up in a pickup truck or semi, she'd have made the invitation without a second thought, had done so, in fact, on several similar occasions. So what stopped her now?

Simple appearance, perhaps? Next to his excellently groomed self, she couldn't help feeling a bit shabby in her well-worn jeans and old work shirt, not to mention the stained apron in which she'd greeted him, but that should not matter. Neither should what this smoothly handsome, well-dressed man would think about the simple apartment behind the unmarked door. The Bible taught that no difference should be made between the wealthy and the poor.

Putting on her smile, Charlotte mentally squared her shoulders and said, "You can eat here. It's just meat loaf tonight, with grilled potatoes, broccoli and greens, but at least none of it's fried."

His relief palpable, he chuckled and spread his arms. "Lead me to it. I'm starving."

Thankful that her brothers hadn't shown up for the evening meal as they did several times a week, she waved him around the end of the counter and indicated the door through which she'd entered. The unexpected company would surprise her grandfather, but she knew that he would be nothing less than gracious. They'd shared their table with hotel guests before, after all, and no doubt would do so again, though they really didn't get all that many strangers stopping in.

They had only twelve rooms, and most of their guests were locals who rented by the month or employees of one of the oil firms that paid handsomely to have rooms constantly available. Several of the truckers who routinely drove along this route stopped in on a weekly basis, usually on Tuesdays or Thursdays, but they didn't get many travelers in this area who weren't there to visit family. Strangers simply had no reason to come, which made her wonder again how Tyler Aldrich happened to be there.

Perhaps he was headed to Duncan and simply hadn't realized how far it could be between gas stations, particularly at night. If Oklahoma City were his destination, surely he'd have used the interstate to the east, while a direct trip to Lawton would have taken him through Wichita Falls. All four cities, she knew for a fact, had Aldrich Grocery stores.

Or maybe he wasn't connected to Aldrich Grocery at all.

What mattered was that he needed a little hospitality, and hospitality, as Granddad would say, was the Jefford family business. More than that, the Lord commanded it in one of Charlotte's favorite passages from the twenty-fifth chapter of Matthew.

Feeding the hungry, giving drink to the thirsty and inviting in the stranger were tenets upon which her grandparents had built their lives as well as their business. She sincerely tried to follow the example set by those two godly people. She'd just never dreamed that would mean inviting a rich man to her humble table.

Chapter Two

Tyler slipped around the end of the counter, quickly falling in behind his unexpected hostess, unexpected in more ways than one. Charlotte Jefford surprised him, not only with her pure, wholesome beauty and wit but with her warmth. He had not intended to spend the night in this place, but since he must he might as well enjoy himself.

Expecting to enter a small coffee shop or café through that private door, he felt momentarily disoriented to find himself standing in what appeared to be a dining room. For one long, awkward moment, he could do nothing more than try to take in the place.

Despite the lack of windows, the light seemed softer, warmer somehow, so that the room came across as homey and intimate if somewhat shabby. An old-fashioned maple dining set with five chairs occupied the greater portion of the room. A sixth chair stood between an overflowing bookcase and the door through which they had just entered.

Three more doors opened off the far wall, all closed at the moment, but Tyler's attention focused on the old man who sat at one end of the oval dining table. As he bent his head over a Bible on the flowered, quilted place mat, his thinning white hair showed a freckled scalp, leaving the impression that he had once been a redhead. He looked up when Charlotte spoke, his faded green eyes owlish beneath a thick pair of glasses, which he immediately removed.

"This is my grandfather."

At the sight of Tyler, surprise flitted across the old man's lean, craggy face, replaced at once by a welcoming smile. Rising in a slow, laborious motion, he put out his hand. Tall and lean but stooped and somewhat frail, he wore a plaid shirt beneath denim bib overalls.

"Hap Jefford," he said in a gravelly voice. "How d'you do."

Tyler leaned forward to shake hands, careful not to grip those gnarled fingers too tightly.

"Tyler Aldrich. Pleased to make your acquaintance." Looking helplessly to Charlotte, who moved past the table toward the kitchen beyond, Tyler tamped down his unease and forced a smile. "I'm, uh, afraid I misunderstood the situation. I thought you had some sort of little restaurant back here."

"Goodness, no," Hap Jefford said with mild

amusement, lowering himself back down onto his seat. He waved toward the chair on his left, indicating that Tyler should also sit. "Eating places are real workhouses. Time was my Lydia thought putting in a restaurant the thing to do, back when we were young enough to hold up and it seemed our boy might join the business here." Hap shook his head, adding, "Not to be. They're both gone to the Lord now. Him first, God rest him."

Tyler hardly knew what to say to that, so he pulled out the chair and sat, nodding sagely. After a moment, he went back to the problem at hand.

"I really don't want to intrude. When your granddaughter said I could eat here, I naturally thought—"

"Oh, don't worry," Hap interrupted. "We got plenty. She always cooks so her brothers can eat if they're of a mind. Evenings when one or the other don't drop by, we have to eat the leftovers for lunch the next day."

Tyler relaxed a bit. "Sounds as if you don't much care for leftovers."

Hap grinned, displaying a finely crafted set of dentures. "Now, I never said that. Charlotte's a right fine cook. I just don't mind a little unexpected change from time to time."

Tyler laughed. "I can understand that."

"How 'bout yourself?" Hap asked conversationally.

Not at all sure how to answer that, Tyler shifted

uncomfortably. "Are you asking how I feel about leftovers or change?"

"Start with the leftovers."

Tyler had to think about that. "I don't think I've ever actually had leftovers as such."

Hap seemed shocked, but then he shook his head, grinning. "Where're you from, boy?"

"Dallas."

"Now, I'd have thought they had leftovers in Dallas," Hap quipped.

Charlotte entered just then with plates, flatware and paper napkins. Hap closed the Bible and set it aside.

"Won't be long now," she announced, placing a delicate flowered plate on the flowered mat in front of Hap. She placed another in front of Tyler.

"You really don't have to feed me," Tyler said uncomfortably as she set the third plate on the mat to Hap's right.

"Don't be silly." She reached across the table to deal out case knives. "It's ready. You're hungry. Might as well eat."

Tyler sensed that declining or offering to pay would insult both of the Jeffords, so he watched silently as she passed out forks and napkins, leaving a stack of the latter on the table.

"Iced tea or water?" she asked. "Tea's sweet, by the way."

"Water," Hap answered. Glancing at Tyler, he added, "Don't need no caffeine this time of evening."

"Water," Tyler agreed, hoping it was bottled.

"I'll be right back."

"Don't forget the ketchup," Hap called as she hurried away.

"As if," came the airy reply.

"Her grandma thought ketchup was an insult to her cooking," Hap confided to Tyler.

"It is when you put it on everything on your plate," Charlotte chided gently, returning from the kitchen with glassware and a pitcher of iced water.

"Oh, I just put it on my taters and meat loaf," Hap said with a good-natured wink at Tyler.

"And your eggs and your steak…" Charlotte retorted, placing the items on the table and moving away again "…red beans, fish, pork chops…" She stopped in the open doorway and turned to address Tyler. "He'll put it on white bread and eat that if there's nothing else on hand."

"That reminds me," Hap said with a wink at Tyler. "Don't forget the bread."

Charlotte gave him a speaking look and disappeared, returning moments later with a half-empty bottle of ketchup and a loaf of sliced bread in a plastic sleeve. She placed both on the table and went away without a word, but the twinkle in her eye bespoke indulgence and amusement.

"Thank you kindly, sugar," Hap called at her receding back. Smiling broadly, he proceeded to open the plastic and take out a slice of bread, squeeze ketchup onto the slice and fold it over before biting off half of it.

Tyler would have winced if his attention hadn't been snagged by something else. The bread wrapper bore the Rich Foods label, the private label of the Aldrich Grocery chain. Aldrich & Associates Grocery had several stores in Oklahoma, of course, and distributed some foodstuffs to independents, but seeing that label there distressed him. It took only a moment to realize why.

He didn't want the Jeffords to connect him with the Aldrich family who owned the grocery chain. He didn't see why they should, really. They might not even know that the Rich Foods brand belonged to the Aldrich Grocery chain, but it seemed very important suddenly that they not make the connection.

All his life, he'd had to worry whether he was liked for himself or his family position. Just once he wanted to know that someone could be nice to him without first calculating what it might be worth. He couldn't even remember the last time anyone had invited him, on the spur of the moment, to share a simple meal for which he was not even expected to pay.

Stunned by the abrupt longing, Tyler spread his hands on his thighs and smiled with false serenity as Hap licked ketchup off his fingers, his expression one of sublime enjoyment. When was the last time, Tyler wondered, that he had enjoyed something that much, especially something so basic?

Charlotte came in again, wearing heavy mitts this time and carrying a casserole dish. When she lifted the lid on that casserole, a meaty aroma filled the room, making Tyler's mouth water and his stomach rumble demandingly. Given a choice in the matter, he never ate meat loaf. Ground beef, in his estimation, rarely constituted healthy eating. But what choice did he have?

She brought the rest of the meal in two trips: crisp round slices of browned potato with the red skins still on, steaming broccoli and a dish of dark greens dotted with onion and bits of bacon. Simple fare, indeed, but Tyler could not remember ever being quite so hungry. Intent on the food, he startled when Hap spoke.

"Heavenly Father…"

Tyler looked up to see Charlotte and Hap with hands linked and heads bowed in prayer. Stunned, he could only sit and stare in uneasy silence.

"We thank You for Your generosity and for our guest. Bless the hands that prepared this meal and the food to the nourishment of our bodies, that we might be strengthened to perform Your will. In Jesus' name. Amen."

"Amen," Charlotte echoed, lifting her head.

Tyler gulped when her gaze collided with his. Belatedly, he realized that she had reached out to offer him a small spatula. When it finally dawned on him that she expected him to serve himself, he shook his head.

"Oh, uh, ladies first."

Smiling, she began to cut the meatloaf into

wedges. Not one to stand on ceremony, Hap dug into the potatoes and plunked the platter down in front of Tyler, reaching for the ketchup. After a moment hunger trumped discomfort, and Tyler began to gingerly fill his plate.

Everything looked, smelled and, to his surprise, tasted delicious. The greens took a little getting used to, but the broccoli and seasoned potatoes were wonderful, and that was saying something, given that he employed an expensive chef and routinely dined in the finest restaurants to be found. The meat loaf, however, came as the biggest surprise.

Melt-in-the-mouth tender with a beguiling blend of flavors, it whet his appetite to a greedy fever pitch. He ate with unaccustomed gusto, and only with gritted teeth did he find enough discipline to forgo a third helping. Hap apparently possessed no such compunction, but as he reached for that third wedge, Charlotte spoke up.

"Pity no one's found a way to take the cholesterol out of beef. You can cook as lean as possible, but there's still that."

Hap subsided with a sigh. Looking to Tyler he commented wryly, "I keep telling her that no one lives forever in this world, but it seems she's in no hurry to see me off to the next." Charlotte made no comment to that, just smiled sweetly. "My first mistake," Hap went on, "was letting her take me to the doctor."

"Mmm. Guess you could've hitchhiked," she commented calmly.

Tyler found himself chuckling as Hap latched onto that gentle riposte with clownish fervor, drawing himself up straight in his chair. "You don't think some sweet young thing would come along and take me up, then?"

Charlotte looked at Tyler and blandly said, "If she happened to be driving an ambulance."

Laughter spilled out of the two men, unrestrained and joyous. Tyler laughed, in fact, until tears clouded his eyes. Whatever clever rejoinder Hap might have made derailed when the door to the lobby opened and two more elderly men strolled in.

"Y'all are having fun without us," one of them accused good-naturedly.

Hap introduced them as Grover Waller and Justus Inman. A third man identified as Teddy Booker called from the outer room, "I'm stoking this here stove. These dominoes are cold as ice!"

Hap got to his feet, eagerness lending speed if not agility to his movements. "You play dominoes, Tyler?"

"No, sir, I'm afraid not."

"You all go on," Charlotte said, "and don't stay up too late. I'll heat up some cider after a while."

"We'll be having some popcorn, too," Hap decided.

"I was hoping for carrot cake," Grover Waller said at just a notch above a whine.

"Now, Pastor," Charlotte told him, "you know you have to watch your sugar."

A belly as round as a beach ball, thin, steel-gray hair sticking out above his ears in tufts and brown eyes twinkling behind wire-rimmed glasses gave the preacher a jovial appearance that belied the mournful tone of his voice as he complained, "You've been talking to my wife."

"And she says you've got to lose twenty pounds or go back on meds," Charlotte confirmed.

He thinned his somewhat fleshy lips and hitched up the waist of his nondescript gray slacks before turning away with a sigh.

"Oh, the burden of a caring wife," Hap intoned, following the two men from the room.

"Seems to me you used to call it meddling," someone said.

"We all do until they're gone," another gravelly voice put in before the door closed behind them.

Charlotte shook her head, smiling. "They're all widowers except for the pastor," she explained. Tyler didn't know what to say to that, so he simply nodded. "They live to play dominoes, those four, and really, what else have they got to do? Well, three of them, anyway. Pastor Waller's nearly twenty years younger than the others, and he's got the church."

"I see."

After an awkward moment of silence, she rose and began to clear the table, saying, "Just let me put these in the kitchen and I'll point you to your room."

The idea of going off alone to a cold, less than

sumptuous room did not appeal to Tyler. Rising, he heard himself say, "Can't I help you clean up?"

He didn't know which of them seemed more surprised. After a moment, Charlotte looked down at the soiled dishes in her arms.

"It's the least I can do after such a fine meal," Tyler pressed, realizing that he hadn't even complimented the cook.

"I suppose your wife expects you to help out at home," she began, shaking her head, "but it's not necessary here."

"No," he denied automatically. "That is, no wife."

"Ah." Charlotte ducked her head shyly. "Well, if it'll make you feel better to help out…"

"Oh, it will," he said, lifting a dish in each hand and following her toward the kitchen. "I never expected a home-cooked meal, especially not such a healthy one." She looked back over her shoulder at that, just before disappearing into the other room. "And tasty," he added quickly, raising his voice. "Very tasty. Delicious, even."

Hearing her wry "Thanks," he stepped into a narrow room with doors at either end.

Countertops of industrial-grade metal contrasted sharply with light green walls and cabinets constructed of pale, golden wood. The white cooking range in the corner by what must have been the outside door looked as if it came straight from the 1950s, while the olive-green refrigerator at the opposite end of the room appeared slightly newer.

Tyler noted with some relief that a modern thermo-stat for a central air-conditioning system had been mounted above the light switch on one wall. He hoped the rooms were similarly equipped.

What he did not see was a dishwasher. It came as no surprise, then, when Charlotte set down the dishes and started running hot water into the sink below the only window he had yet seen in the small apartment. Covered with frilly, translucent curtains in yellow trimmed with green, that window looked out over a small patio lit by a single outdoor light. Leaves swirled across the patterned brick, snagging on the thin legs of wrought-iron furniture in need of a new coat of green paint.

"You can put those down there," Charlotte said, indicating the counter with a tilt of her head.

Hurrying to do as instructed, Tyler looked up to find her tying that white apron around her impos-sibly narrow waist again. Quickly switching his gaze, he watched suds foam up beneath the running water as she squeezed in detergent.

"Better take your coat off," she advised.

He did that, then looked around for someplace to hang it before walking back into the other room to drape it over a chair. It only seemed sensible to pick up the remaining dishes before heading back to the kitchen.

Returning, he found that Charlotte had already made order out of chaos, stacking the dirty dishes as they were evidently to be washed. Glassware came first, followed by plates, flatware, serving dishes, utensils and finally pans. The leftover food had disappeared into the refrigerator, from which she turned as he entered the narrow room.

"I'll take those," she said, coming forward.

He surrendered the two plates and platter, then watched her scrape food scraps into a bucket beneath the sink, which she then sealed with a tightly fitting lid before stacking the dishes with the others. Turning, she placed her back to the counter, her gaze falling to the neatly cuffed sleeves of his stark-white shirt. Her mouth gave a little quirk at one corner as she reached for a pair of yellow vinyl gloves and pulled them on.

Wordlessly, she turned to the sink now billowing with suds, and reached for a plate on the stack to her right. While she washed and rinsed, Tyler wandered haplessly across the room, taking in a calendar from a local propane company on the side of the refrigerator and a clock shaped like a rooster over the stove. When he turned he saw a cookie jar in the form of an owl on the opposite counter next to a small microwave and a glass-domed container covering three layers of a dark, rich, grainy cake iced with frothy white. Several pieces had already been cut from it.

"Is that carrot cake?" he asked.

She sent him an amused glance. "Of course. Want a piece?"

A hand strayed to his flat middle, but thinking of the extra time on the treadmill required to work that off, he said, "Better not."

She hitched a shoulder, handing him a wet plate with one hand and a striped towel with the other. Tyler had hold of them before he knew what was happening, but then he just stood there, confused and out of place.

Plunging her hands back into the soapy water, she asked smoothly, "Are you going to dry that or just let it drip all over those expensive shoes?"

He looked down, saw the dark droplets shining on black Italian leather and quickly put the towel to good use.

"That dish goes in the cabinet behind you," she told him, a hint of amusement in her tone. "Door on the far right."

Stepping across the room, he opened the cabinet, found an empty vertical space separated by dowels and slid the dish into it, noting that two sets of dishes were stored there, cheap dark brown stoneware, chipped in places, and the poor-quality flowered china from which he had eaten.

He realized at once that she had served him from her good plates. Both embarrassed and gratified, he left the door open and went back for more plates. A short stack of clean, wet dishes stood on the metal countertop beside the sink.

"Looks like I'm behind," he admitted unashamedly. "But then, I've never done this before."

She smiled and added another dish to the pile. "I know."

Laughing, he got to work, making small talk as

he dried and shelved the dishes. "How does a woman such as yourself come to be working in a motel?"

Looking out the window, she replied matter-of-factly, "Her parents die and she winds up living with her grandparents, who just happen to own and operate that motel."

"My condolences," he offered softly.

"It happened a long time ago," she replied evenly, glancing at him. "I was fourteen."

"Eons ago, obviously," he teased, hoping to lighten the mood. She ducked her head.

"Thirteen years."

That would make her twenty-seven, he calculated, a good age. He remembered it well. Had it only been eight years ago? At the time it had seemed that thirty would never come and his father would live forever. Yet, Comstock Aldrich had died of pancreatic cancer only nine months ago, leaving Tyler to fill his gargantuan shoes at Aldrich & Associates. After only ten months in the job, Tyler felt old and burdened, while Charlotte Jefford seemed refreshingly young and...serene.

He blinked at that, realizing just how much that calm serenity appealed to him. It fairly radiated from her pores.

"What about you?" she asked.

He studiously did not look at her. "Oh, I'm thirty-five, an executive, nothing you'd find interesting, I'm sure. You mentioned brothers. Older or younger?"

A slight pause made him wonder if she knew that he'd purposefully been less than forthcoming. "Older. Holt's thirty-six, and Ryan's thirty-four. Holt was working in the city when our folks passed, and Ryan was in college, so naturally I came here."

"The city?"

"Oklahoma City."

"Ah. And these brothers of yours, what do they do?"

"Well, Holt is a driller, like our daddy was. The price of oil these days keeps him pretty busy. He's got a little ranch east of town, too. I can't help worrying some, because that's how Daddy died." She looked down at her busy hands, adding softly, "He fell from a derrick." An instant later, she seemed to throw off the melancholy memory. "But everything's more modern now, safer, or so Holt says."

"I see."

"Ryan," she went on, warming to her subject, "he's the assistant principal at the high school. He teaches history, too, and coaches just about every sport they offer. Football, baseball, basketball, volleyball, even track." She gave Tyler a look, saying, "In a small town, you have to do it all."

"Sounds like it."

"Do you have brothers and sisters?" she asked.

"One of each. She's older. He's younger." *And they hate my guts,* Tyler thought, surprised by a stab of regret.

"Children?"

He shook his head. "Never married."

"Oh. Me, neither." She shrugged. "You know how it is in a small town, slim pickings."

He actually didn't know, and he didn't care to know. What he did care about surprised him. Put plainly, he wanted her to like him. He wanted her to like him for himself, not for social status or wealth or any of the other reasons for which everyone else liked him, because he could give them things, because his last name happened to be Aldrich.

For the first time in his life, it mattered what someone thought of him, someone who didn't know the Aldrich family, someone without the least claim to influence or wealth, someone willing to invite him, a stranger, to dinner. Someone who would take him at face value.

It mattered, even if he couldn't figure out why.

Charlotte saw her guest to the kitchen door, which opened on the same side of the building as the drive-through, and pointed across the way to his room. After thanking her profusely for the meal, he walked toward his car. Looking in that direction through the screen, she recognized her brother Holt's late-model, double-cab pickup truck as it turned into the motel lot. The truck swung to the left and stopped nose-in at the end of the building next to the pastor's sedan.

"You're late," she called as he stepped down from the cab, his gaze aimed at the man now dropping down behind the driver's wheel of that expensive sports car. Still wearing his work clothes, greasy denim jeans and jacket over a simple gray undershirt, Holt had at least traded his grimy steel-toed boots for his round-toed, everyday cowboy pair.

Tall and lean, Holt took a great deal after their grandfather in appearance, though with different coloring. A lock of his thick, somewhat shaggy, sandy-brown hair fell over one vibrant green eye, and he impatiently shoved it back with a large, calloused, capable hand as bronzed by the sun as his face was. His long legs and big, booted feet ate up the ground as he strode toward her.

"Who's that?" he asked, pulling wide the screen door and following her into the kitchen.

"Name's Tyler Aldrich," she answered. "I'm pretty sure he's one of the Aldrich grocery store family."

Holt lifted an eyebrow. "What gives you that idea?"

"Just a hunch."

She liked to shop at an Aldrich store and had often driven as far as fifty miles to do so. More than once she'd seen the large photograph of an older man identified as Comstock Aldrich affixed to a wall over the motto, From Our Family To Yours. She couldn't remember enough about that man's face to say whether or not Tyler resembled him in any way, but she'd seen the way Tyler had reacted when she'd plopped that loaf of bread on the table.

Normally, with a guest in attendance, she made hot bread or at least served the sliced variety stacked on a pretty saucer. Tonight she'd left that bread in its wrapper just to see what he would do. He'd stared as if he'd thought the thing might pop up, point a floury finger and identify him.

"Supposing he is who you think he is, what's he doing here?" Holt asked, going to the refrigerator to take out the plate of leftovers she'd stowed there earlier. "You reckon he's going to open a store hereabouts? That'd be cool."

Charlotte frowned. She hadn't thought of that possibility. After all, he'd said he was stranded, and she had no reason to doubt him. Except that just then he drove by in that flashy car of his. Apparently he had *some* gas. She turned to look at her brother, who carried the food to the microwave and set the timer.

"An Aldrich store might be very welcome," she said, "unless you're Stu Booker."

Stu had taken over the local grocery from his father, Teddy, who sat at the domino table in the front room with Hap at that very moment.

Holt turned to lean against the counter. "I see what you mean. Another grocery would put Booker's out of business." The microwave dinged, and Holt reached inside to remove the plate, asking, "Still got that carrot cake, I see."

"Yes," Charlotte muttered, "but you'll have to eat it in here. Grover's playing dominoes tonight."

Nodding, Holt took a fork from the drawer and strolled into the other room and toward the lobby, his big boots clumping on the bare floor. "I'll be back, then. Thanks, sis."

"Welcome," she answered automatically, her mind on other matters.

Should Aldrich Grocery put in a store here, the Bookers would undoubtedly suffer. It was, she decided, a matter for prayer. And perhaps a bit of subtle investigation.

Chapter Three

Charlotte glanced at her watch, more than a little miffed.

On weekdays, she started cleaning the rooms as soon as the oil-field workers left in the mornings and by this time usually could be sitting down to lunch with her grandfather. On Saturdays, she got a later start because the workmen liked to sleep in a bit before heading home to their families. Lunch, therefore, came later on Saturdays, but not normally this late.

It was already past twelve, and she still had one room left to do before she could begin preparing the midday meal, thanks to Tyler Aldrich. On a few occasions she'd had to put off the cleaning until the afternoon, but that pushed her workday well into the night as she had a weekly chore scheduled for each afternoon.

Saturday afternoons were reserved for washing

and rehanging drapes. If she didn't do at least three sets of drapes each week, she'd either be a week behind or have to do it on Monday, the day she shampooed carpets. Tuesday afternoons were dedicated to outside windows, Wednesdays to replacing shower curtains, Thursdays to cleaning oil stains off the pavement and policing the grounds. Fridays she cleaned the lobby top to bottom and did the shopping.

In this fashion, she not only cleaned every occupied room each day, she completely freshened every room once a month, while maintaining the lobby and grounds on a weekly basis and keeping their storeroom stocked. Hap did his part by handling the registration desk and banking, balancing the books, ordering supplies and helping out with the daily laundry.

She did not appreciate having her carefully balanced schedule upset. Obviously, the man had no idea what it took to keep an operation like this running smoothly. Then again, few folks did. Deciding that she was being unfair, she left the service cart on the walkway in front of number eight and rapped her knuckles on the door. She began slowly counting to ten, intending to walk away if he hadn't answered by then. She'd reached seven before the door wrenched open.

Tyler Aldrich stood there in his bare feet, rumpled slacks and a half-buttoned shirt, looking harried and irritated, his dark hair ruffled. A day's growth of chocolate beard shadowed his face. If she'd had to guess, she'd have said he hadn't slept very well.

He wrinkled his face at the glare of the sun and demanded, "What *is* that noise?"

"Noise?" She glanced around in puzzlement.

He put a hand to his head. "Ka-shunk, ka-shunk. All night long."

"Oh, that noise. There's a pump jack out back."

He sighed. "Of course. Oil pumps. Should've figured that one."

"I'm so used to the sound, I don't even notice it anymore," she admitted, "but we don't get many complaints about it." They hadn't actually had any complaints about it until now.

"I don't suppose it would bother me if it wasn't so quiet around here," he grumbled.

Well, which is it, she wondered, saying nothing, *too quiet or too noisy?*

He put a hand to the back of his neck. "Didn't think I'd ever get to sleep, especially after those two fellows showed up about midnight."

"What two fellows?"

He waved a hand at that. "Roadside service sent them. I called before I stopped in here. Then after I decided to stay, I forgot to call back and tell them not to bother bringing me gas."

"They came at that time of night just to bring you gas?" she asked in disbelief.

"A few gallons," he muttered. "I still have to fill up."

She shook her head. The rich really did live differently than everyone else. "I hate to be an inconvenience, but I need to clean this room before I feed Granddad."

Nodding, he hid a yawn behind one hand. "Yeah, okay, just give me a few minutes to get out of your way."

"I'll be right here when you're ready," she told him politely, linking her hands behind her back. No way was she going away again. Experience had taught her that a guest would just head straight back to bed and she'd have this exercise to repeat.

Tyler gave her a lopsided grin. "Swell. Uh, listen, can I get breakfast at that café downtown?"

"Sure," she answered, and then for some reason she couldn't begin to fathom she went on. "But if you're willing to settle for lunch, you can eat with us again."

He stopped rubbing his eyes long enough to stare at her, his brow beetled. "Lunch?"

Wondering why she'd issued the invitation, she hastily backtracked as far as good manners would allow. "Just sandwiches, I'm afraid. I don't have time for anything else."

"What time is it, anyway?"

She didn't even have to look. "About ten minutes past noon."

Tyler goggled his eyes. "Noon? You're sure?" She held up her wrist, just in case he wanted to check for himself. His sky-blue eyes closed as he turned away. "I must've slept a lot better than I thought."

"You mean you're not used to sleeping till noon?" She clapped a hand over her mouth, shocked at herself. She never made unwarranted assumptions about people. Well, hardly ever. Fortunately he had not noticed.

"Not anymore," he muttered enigmatically, looking for something. Finding it, he hurried over to snatch his footwear from the floor beside the low dresser that held the television set. Plopping down in the chair that pulled out from the small desk in front of the window, he began yanking on his socks. "Sorry about this. I'll get out now and let you clean."

"No problem."

"Say, is there someplace I can buy a toothbrush and shaving gear?" he asked, rising to stomp into his shoes.

She hesitated a moment before telling him, but really, what harm could it do? "Booker's will have everything you need. Just go out here and turn right." She pointed behind her. "They're a block east of downtown."

Nodding, he stuffed in his shirttail and reached for his suit jacket. "Thanks."

He started toward her, then stopped and went back to snatch his wallet and keys from the bedside table attached to the wall. With a glance in her direction, he picked up the room key and pocketed that, too.

Did he intend to stay another night? That didn't seem like the behavior of a man who just happened to have gotten stranded by an empty gas tank. On the other hand, he'd obviously been unprepared to stay. Maybe he just needed someplace to clean up before he headed out of town. Knowing that she should give him the benefit of the doubt, she backed up as he came through the door.

He went to his car while she maneuvered the service cart into the room. A moment after that, the low-slung car rumbled to life.

She whispered a prayer as she stripped the sheets from the bed. "He's not a bad sort, Lord, but the Bookers have been here a long time, generations, and I know You look after Your own."

For the first time, she wondered if Tyler Aldrich, too, could be a believer. A shiver of…something… went through her, something too foolish to even ponder.

"Well, hello, there! Abe Houton."

For at least the fourth time in the space of the past ten minutes, Tyler put down what could well be the best, not to mention the cheapest, cup of coffee he'd ever tasted in order to shake the hand of a stranger. Dallas owned a reputation as a friendly city, Tyler mused, but tiny Eden, Oklahoma, put it to ridiculous shame.

He cleared his throat, managed a brief smile and returned the greeting. "Tyler Aldrich."

Built like a fireplug, short and squat, Abe Houton sported a fine handlebar mustache that would have made Wyatt Earp as proud as the tall brown beaver cowboy hat poised on Houton's bald head.

"Good to meet you, Tyler. Welcome to Eden. Haven't seen you around here before. What brings you to town?"

Tyler would have wondered if the shield pinned to Abe Houton's white, Western-style shirt had more to do with the question than simple friendliness but for the fact that he'd been asked the same thing repeatedly since he'd come into the Garden of Eden café. And he hadn't even had his buckwheat flapjacks yet.

When he'd sat down at this small, square table in the window, he'd intended to fill his time with people-watching while he dined on an egg-white omelet or a nice bagel with fat-free cream cheese and fruit. Unfortunately he'd become the center of attention for everyone who passed by and the healthiest breakfast he could come up with from the menu was whole-grain flapjacks. The forty-something waitress with the hairnet had openly gaped when he'd asked her to hold the butter and inquired about organic maple syrup.

Tyler looked the local policeman in the eye and repeated words he'd already said so many times that they were ringing in his ears. "Just passing through."

"Aw, that's too bad," the diminutive lawman

remarked, sounding as if he meant it. "This here is a right fine town."

Tyler sat back against the speckled, off-white vinyl that padded the black, steel-framed chairs clustered around the red-topped tables. A floor of black-painted concrete and, oddly enough, knotty pine walls provided the backdrop. What really caught the eye, though, was the old-fashioned soda fountain behind the counter.

"I hope you don't mind if I ask what's so special about this town," Tyler said, truly curious.

Houton rocked back on the substantial heels of his sharp-toed brown cowboy boots, one stubby hand adjusting the small holster on his belt. The pistol snapped inside looked like a toy. Then again, Houton himself resembled a stuffed doll. Tyler had to wonder just how lethal either might be.

"Why, this is Eden, son," the little man declared, as if that answered everything. Then, with unabashed enthusiasm he added, "You should see our park."

"You mean the park at the end of the street?"

"So you have seen it! Bet you didn't notice the footbridge. My daddy helped build that footbridge out of old train rails. Prettiest little footbridge you'll ever see. Really, you should stop by and take a look."

Tyler didn't know whether to laugh or run out and take a look at this local wonder. Fortunately, the waitress arrived just then with his flapjacks, along with a dish of mixed berries, a jug of something that passed for syrup and a refill of aromatic coffee. Houton excused himself with a doff of his hat to straddle a stool at the counter, his feet barely reaching the floor.

Lifting the top edge of a suspiciously tall stack, Tyler saw that succulent slices of ham had been sandwiched between the airy brown flapjacks. A sane, sensible, health-conscious man would remove the meat. A hungry man would just dive in. A self-indulgent one would pour on the so-called syrup and enjoy. Tyler reached for the jug, thinking that he had nothing better to do all day than work off a few extra calories.

An unexpected sense of freedom filled him as he watched the thick, golden-brown liquid flow down. Maybe, he thought, surprising himself, he'd even check out the park.

Nearly half an hour later, Tyler made his way out of the small café, nodding over his shoulder at those who called farewells in his wake. Stuffed to the gills and ridiculously happy about it, he decided that he might as well walk off some of what he'd just consumed and left the car sitting in the slanted space across the street where he'd parked it in front of a resale shop. Hands in his pockets, he strolled along the broad, street-level sidewalk, nodding at those who nodded at him in greeting, which was everyone he encountered. Even old ladies driving—or, more accurately, creeping—down the street in their pristine ten- or twenty-year-old cars waved at him. Tyler nodded back and kept an eye peeled for someplace to work up a good sweat.

He came rather quickly to the park and spied at a distance the aforementioned footbridge spanning the creek that bisected the gently rolling lawn studded with brightly leaved trees. Erosion from the banks of the creek colored the shallow water redorange, which seemed oddly apt in this autumn setting.

Concrete benches scattered beneath the trees invited him to sit for a spell, but he resisted the urge. Picnic tables clustered in one section of the broad space.

A few children and a pair of adult women peopled a playground near the small parking area, where carelessly dropped bicycles awaited their young riders. Tyler turned away, wondering what he was doing in Eden, Oklahoma. He pondered that as he strolled back toward his car.

A plump woman in baggy jeans and an oversize sweater swept leaves off the sidewalk in front of a small white clapboard church on the corner nearest the park. Tyler thought he recognized the sedan parked in front of the modest brick house beside it as one he'd seen at the motel last night, but he couldn't be sure. Walking on he realized that the boxy two-story building behind the church actually belonged to it, easily tripling the building's size.

He got in the car and set off to purchase toiletries,

taking in the town along the way. All of Eden had been laid out in neat, square blocks that made navigation laughably simple. Turning off Garden Avenue, he meandered along Elm and Ash streets. Elm offered primarily commercial buildings, but Ash hosted the most substantial homes he'd yet seen. Constructed of brick and mottled stone, most with square or round pillars supporting deep, broad porches, none could be described as stately and all dated from the 1920s and '30s.

Noting that he'd driven into town on Pecan, he wondered if all the streets were named for trees. Turning on the GPS, he sat with the engine idling at a stop sign long enough to study a city map. It turned out that only the streets running east and west were named for trees. The streets running north and south were named for flowers. He smiled at such fanciful monikers as Lilac, Sunflower, Iris and Snapdragon.

Marveling at the neatness and simplicity of the city scheme, he looked up. A check of his rearview mirror revealed an SUV queued up behind him. He had no idea how long it had been there, but instead of blaring the horn, as any driver in Dallas would have done instantly, the frothy-haired woman behind the wheel gave him a cheery wave. Saluting in apology, Tyler pulled out and made his way to Booker's.

The store fascinated him. Occupying a former ice house, it served as a historical microcosm of progress over the past half century, with goods ranging from a fair but mundane selection of groceries to cosmetics and cheap bedroom slippers.

He bought the necessary items, paying cash, before taking himself back to the motel, where he shaved and brushed his teeth. He put off showering in hopes of finding an adequate health club somewhere close by. Relishing the thought of working himself into a state of sweaty exhaustion, he walked over to the motel lobby in search of information.

Charlotte adjusted the heat on the heavy-duty clothes drier, set the timer on her watch, checked the load in the washer and walked back into the apartment through the door that opened from the laundry room to the kitchen. Moving swiftly, she passed through the dining room and on into the reception area. With Hap and his buddies at the domino table, she need not worry about having the front desk staffed and so turned at once toward the office. A familiar voice stopped her in her tracks.

"I wonder if you gentlemen might tell me where I can find some workout clothes and a gym?"

Laughter erupted.

Rolling her eyes, Charlotte moved at once to the counter. Justus had all but fallen off his chair, while Teddy and Hap tried to maintain some semblance of good manners, without much success. Tyler stood before the game table, his hands in the pockets of his pants as he waited stoically for their amusement to die away. At length, Hap cleared his throat.

"Only gym hereabouts is down to the high school, son."

"If you're wanting a good workout, though, you can get that out at my place," Justus teased. "I got about a hunerd head of cattle what need feeding and a barnyard full of hay ready for storage. Keys are in the tractor."

Justus chortled at his own joke, while Teddy snickered and Hap kept clearing his throat in a belated effort to remain impassive. Torn between amusement and pity, Charlotte leaned both elbows on the counter and interjected herself into the conversation.

"He looks like he's in pretty good shape to me, Justus. You never can tell, Tyler might be able to shift those big old round hay bales without a tractor."

Tyler shot her a wry, grateful look over one shoulder.

"He could get one on each end of a metal bar and lift 'em like weights," Teddy suggested with a big grin.

"Speaking of weights," Charlotte went on, addressing Tyler directly as he turned to face her. "If that's what you're interested in, I could always call my brother. He could get you into the field house."

"That would be, um, Holt?"

"Ryan. Holt's the older one."

Tyler nodded. "The driller. Among other things."

Uncomfortably aware that the other three men were suddenly listening avidly, Charlotte kept her tone light. "Exactly. Ryan's the coach—"

"History teacher, assistant principal," Tyler finished for her. "I wouldn't want to put him out."

"Well, he's your best bet," she said a bit more smartly than she'd intended. "Nearest health club is around fifty miles from here."

Tyler looked lost for a moment. Then Hap laid down his dominoes. "Here now. We could use a fourth for forty-two. Straight dominoes has me bored to tears. You wouldn't consider sitting in, would you? Least ways until Grover finishes his sermon for tomorrow."

Tyler shifted his weight from foot to foot. "I don't know how to play forty-two."

"Oh, we'll teach you," volunteered Justus, as if making amends for his teasing earlier. "Won't we, Teddy?"

"Sure thing. He can play opposite Hap."

To Charlotte's surprise, Tyler pulled out the empty chair at the table. "Does that mean we're partners?"

"That's what it means," Hap answered, obviously pleased that he'd picked up on that. Hap began turning the dominoes facedown and mixing them up. "Since I'm paired with the new kid, I get first shake." He looked to Tyler, instructing, "Now draw seven."

Hanging over the counter, her chin balanced on the heel of her hand, Charlotte got caught up in the game. She jerked when her timer beeped. By then, Tyler had learned enough to engage in a bidding war with Justus. Ill-advised, perhaps, but gutsy.

"Two marks."

"Three."

"You don't even know what you're doing," Justus warned.

"Then your partner can take me off."

"I'm not bidding four marks. You two are nuts."

Charlotte laughed as she slipped through the door into the apartment, hearing Hap declare, "Lead 'em, partner. I got your off covered."

It wouldn't surprise her one bit if the newbie made his bid and taught a couple of old dogs a new trick or two, but why that should please her so, she couldn't say.

Chapter Four

The sun hung low over the horizon when Charlotte heard footsteps scraping on the pavement. She pulled her bulky, navy-blue cardigan a little tighter and crossed her legs before reaching over to close the Bible on the low, wrought-iron table at her elbow to keep the breeze from ruffling the pages. Picking up her coffee cup, she sipped and smiled with contentment.

This was her favorite time of day. With the work done and Granddad's dinner in the oven, she could steal a few minutes to just sit out on the patio and ponder. What would normally be a moment of supreme relaxation, however, suddenly became tinged with something else as Tyler Aldrich strolled around the corner of the building.

"Hello, there."

She shifted in her seat, uncomfortable with the way he made her feel and a little ashamed for it.

Pushing the unwelcome feelings aside, she smiled in greeting. "Hello, yourself. Game's over, I take it."

He grinned. "Grover just showed up."

"Ah. Lost your seat, then."

"I don't mind. Looks like I found another one." He pointed to the chaise next to her. Like her own chair, it lacked padding and the dark green paint had flecked off in places, but he didn't seem to care. Good manners demanded that she nod, and he sat down sideways, using the elongated seat like a bench. "At least your grandfather didn't seem particularly eager to lose me as a partner."

Charlotte laughed. "He likes to win, and Grover's too polite to trounce the competition. You must've caught on well."

Tyler shrugged. "I have a good head for numbers, and it's a pretty entertaining game. Kind of like bridge. Do you play?"

"Bridge? No. Forty-two, absolutely, but usually just with the family, my brothers, Granddad and me."

"So tell me something. What is nello?" Tyler asked.

Charlotte chuckled. "Am I to understand that they wouldn't let you bid nello?"

"Never came to that. It's just something Grover said as we were playing out my last hand."

She explained that a nello bid meant the exact opposite of a trump bid. Instead of trying to catch enough tricks and count to make the bid, the nello bidder tried not to catch a single trick or point, despite having to lead the first trick.

Tyler nodded with satisfaction. "Makes sense now. I didn't have a domino larger than a trey that last hand."

"And Grover would have seen that. He does love to play nello," Charlotte put in.

Glancing around in the softening light Tyler commented, "I can't remember the last time I spent half the day playing games."

"Sounds like a case of all work and no play to me." She sipped from her mug, realizing belatedly that her hospitality lacked something. She held up the cup. "Care for coffee?"

"Decaf?"

"Sorry, no, but I've got some if you want to wait for it to make."

"Don't bother. I'm pretty content as I am." He leaned back slightly, bracing his palms on the edge of the chaise. "You're one to talk about all work and no play. I never realized how much work even a small motel can be." He waved a hand. "Hap filled me in on some of what you were doing all day."

Had Tyler asked where she was? She tried not to let the possibility feel too good or even think about why it did. This man would be gone tomorrow. Her interest in him was a matter of hospitality, nothing more. Or it should be. She couldn't imagine why it was necessary even to tell herself such things. Hadn't she learned, long ago, that she should live her life without romantic entanglements? In her experience, someone usually got hurt. Once was quite enough for her.

She managed to shrug and say off-handedly, "Well, there's always Sunday. We don't even staff the front desk then. No reason to, really. Our regular trade runs Monday through Friday."

"I'd think traffic would pick up on the weekend," he mused.

"Not really. Most of it's local. A few trucks come through. Not much else."

"Must make for a slow, easy life," he observed.

"Slow, maybe. Easy? Well, that depends."

He nodded. "Right. I wouldn't say that what you do is easy."

"Oh, it's not that hard, especially if you establish a routine. Mostly it's just time-consuming."

"Did you never want to do anything else?" he asked.

She answered without thought. "Not really. I didn't feel called to teach school or what have you. Don't see any point in waiting tables or clerking when I can do this, and trust me, I'd make a lousy secretary." She shook her head. "This always felt right for me."

"I guess your grandfather is happy about that."

"I'm not sure he's really thought about it. He loves this life, and I don't think he ever imagined I wouldn't."

"Do you?"

"Sure. I wasn't certain at first." She shrugged.

"Teenagers just want to be like everyone else, you know, even when they're working so hard to be different, and living in a motel is not the same as living in a house. That bugged me for a while."

Tyler chuckled. "I don't see you as a rebellious teen."

"Not at all," she admitted, "but I had to make my peace with this life. After Gran got sick and her heart weakened, I started taking over more and more of her work, and I had the satisfaction of knowing that it gave her comfort at the end to think Granddad wouldn't be shouldering all this alone."

"I can't imagine that he's up to much of the physical work," Tyler said carefully. "Arthritis?"

"Among other things," she confirmed, "but he doesn't let it get him down."

"Yes, I noticed that. He seems, well, happy. You don't know how lucky you are that he's so upbeat."

"Oh, I'm blessed, and I know it. My mother was just the opposite, you see, always worried, always feeling slighted and threatened. I sometimes don't know what my father saw in her."

"I do," Tyler said softly, "if she looked like you."

Stunned and dangerously thrilled, Charlotte floundered a bit, responding pragmatically to what she knew had not been a strictly practical comment. "Oh. No, actually. Her hair was much darker and…b-blue eyes. She was shorter, too."

His smile tightened. "I mean, she must have been as pretty as you, as wholesomely attractive."

Charlotte gulped. Of course she'd known what he meant, but for some reason she'd made him say it, and now that he had, she felt even more flustered. "Uh, yes. Th-that is, she was quite stunningly beautiful, actually. And I should've said thank you."

"You're welcome." A grin flashed across his face, then he threaded his fingers together around one knee, saying lightly, "Sounds as if you might have had some issues with your mother."

Charlotte ducked her head. Silly of her. It had been so long ago. Still, it was not a pretty story, not one to discuss with the merest acquaintance, anyway, even one who made her want to know him better, *especially* one who made her want to know him better. And especially with a man like him. Rich, probably even spoiled. What could he possibly know or care about her life? She adopted a light, airy tone.

"Doesn't everyone have issues with their mothers?"

He chuckled. "I suppose."

She changed the subject by inviting him to speak about himself. "I seem to recall that you mentioned a brother and sister."

"That's right." Nodding, he named Cassandra, who was just fourteen months older than him, and Preston, twenty-six months younger. "We all work together."

"Really? That sounds like fun."

"Hardly," he scoffed. "All that sibling rivalry

makes for a crazy dynamic, especially since someone has to be the boss."

"And that someone would be you," Charlotte murmured, somehow knowing it.

He leaned forward, forearms against his knees. "That would be me," he admitted, "and my brother and sister both resent it. When they're not fighting with each other or our mother and stepmother, they're ganging up on me."

Charlotte absorbed that for a moment, thankful that she and her brothers had always gotten along quite well, though Holt and Ryan had been known to bicker and quarrel as youngsters. Their father, she recalled, had worked hard to make them friends. Many times he had told them that if they were kind to one another they would be best friends when they grew up. Apparently Tyler's parents had not succeeded in that regard with their children.

"Sounds difficult. I notice you didn't mention your dad."

Tyler clasped his hands. "He died about nine months ago from pancreatic cancer."

Charlotte sat forward. "I am sorry."

"Thanks." He studied her as if trying to decide whether or not she was sincere before adding, "The cancer came suddenly and hit hard. His death changed everything and nothing, if you know what I mean."

Charlotte shook her head, eyebrows drawn together. Her own beloved father's death had changed everything, absolutely everything, in her family's world. She couldn't imagine it being otherwise. "I'm not sure I do."

Tyler spread his hands, looking down at them pensively. "I-I'm not sure I can explain."

"You could try," she prodded gently, sensing that he needed to talk about it.

He sat in silence for so long that she began to feel embarrassed. Then suddenly he spoke.

"My parents divorced when I was twenty-four. I wouldn't say that it was a particularly acrimonious marriage, but no one was really surprised, not even when Dad married his secretary." He speared Charlotte with a glance. "Shasta is only five years older than me, and no one will ever know what she should have looked like, if you follow me."

"I'm assuming there's plastic surgery involved," Charlotte said, disciplining a smile.

"At sixty-one, Mother is a whole lot resentful, not that she hasn't had some tasteful work done herself, you understand."

Charlotte lifted her eyebrows slightly. "Sounds as if you have a very interesting family."

"Interesting I can handle," Tyler muttered, sitting up straight. "The real problem is that ours is a family business, and everyone has seats on the board, along with some longtime employees and investors. My brother and sister and I received shares throughout the years, always on an equal basis, mind you. Mom got hers in the divorce, and Shasta inherited hers when Dad died. Throw in the fact that Dad named me CEO a month before he passed, and it makes for some, shall we say, volatile board meetings." He lifted a hand to the back of his neck, adding, "To tell you the truth, I walked out of one of those meetings yesterday. That's how I wound up here."

"Wow." Charlotte shook her head, half-relieved because Tyler hadn't come to Eden with a mind to put in an Aldrich store, half-sympathetic because his family obviously plagued rather than blessed him. "And everyone thinks that a family with all the advantages of the Aldrich grocery store chain has it made."

Tyler stiffened, a look of such affront and disappointment on his face that Charlotte caught her breath, realizing abruptly how judgmental she must have sounded. Before she could even begin to apologize, he lurched to his feet and stalked away.

For a moment, she could do nothing more than gape at his retreating back. He'd covered about half the distance to his room before she hastily ditched the coffee and leaped up to follow, without even a clue as to what she would say when she caught up to him. If she caught up to him.

He couldn't believe it. There he'd sat thinking that Charlotte Jefford had to be the most refreshing, unassuming, genuine human being he'd ever met, and all along she'd known exactly who he was. She'd probably known from the moment he'd signed the guest registration card.

He had to hand it to her, though. She hadn't let on in any fashion. Not one simpering smile had slipped out, not one admiring titter, not one desperately suggestive whisper. Until the end. Until *after* he'd spilled his guts like some needy guest on one of those tawdry psycho-babble talk shows.

What on earth had gotten into him? He'd never said those things to anyone. Any complaints he made about his personal life had always come back to haunt him. Generally his family would hear of them before the words were out of his mouth, not to mention his rivals.

His circles of acquaintance nurtured some notorious gossips, so he'd learned early on to keep his personal thoughts and feelings to himself. Every word out of his mouth could be, and often was, used against him in some fashion or another. He hadn't realized until just that very moment how confining and…lonely that had become. To his perplexed shame, he'd wanted her to know him, really know him, because somehow Charlotte Jefford had felt *safe*.

Let this be a lesson to him. Not even a quiet, seemingly serene stranger stuck out here in this small town in the middle of nowhere and nothing made a *safe* confidant, not for him, not when she had known who he was all along.

The bitter depth of his disappointment shocked him. She was nothing to him, nothing at all. Yet, he could not deny what he felt. Swamped with angry misery, he did not even hear her run after him, did not hear her calling his name, until she touched him, her hand slipping around to fall on his forearm.

"Tyler!"

He turned back before he could think better of it, and found himself looking down into her troubled hazel eyes. Something wrenched inside him, something frightfully needy. Making a belated attempt to extricate himself, he stepped away. "You'll have to excuse me."

"I'm sorry," she gasped. "I'm so sorry. I'm not usually that blunt or insensitive."

His defenses firmly in place now, a ready, hard-won insouciance surged forward, burying his disillusionment. "I can't imagine what you mean."

She looked crestfallen, ashamed. "I shouldn't have implied that money made you different or could solve all your problems."

"Problems?" he echoed lightly. "What would you know about my problems, anyway?"

He winced inwardly at that last, surprised by the inexplicable need to hurt her. As she, he realized with a jolt, had hurt him.

The wideness of her mottled eyes proclaimed that his jab had hit its mark; the frank, troubled depths of them told him that she would not retaliate in kind, increasing his guilt tenfold in an instant. Like intricate quilts of soft golds, greens and blues those eyes offered comfort and warmth, as well as surprising beauty.

"I'm sorry, Tyler. I—I don't know what else to say."

Anger leaked out of him like air from a balloon.

"No, I'm sorry. I overreacted."

Unable to maintain contact with those eyes, he looked away. The unwelcome feeling that he owed her some explanation pushed words from him.

"How long have you known exactly who I am?"

When she didn't answer immediately, he speared her with an incisive glance. She looked confused.

"You mean when did I put you together with the Aldrich grocery stores?"

"That's exactly what I mean."

She shrugged. "As soon as I learned your name. Why wouldn't I put it together? It's perfectly natural to associate one thing with another. I didn't know for sure, of course, until I saw your reaction to the bread."

"So that was deliberate," he accused, more wounded than indignant.

"Serving the only loaf of bread I had in the house?" she asked plaintively, but then she bit her lip. "No, that's not fair. It was the only loaf, but I did want to see how you'd react."

Sighing, he pinched the bridge of his nose. Could he be a bigger fool? With Aldrich stores blanketing the seven states nearest to Texas, did he really think she wouldn't put it together?

"I won't tell anyone if it's that important to you," she vowed softly.

He nodded, miserable in a way he couldn't explain even to himself. "Yeah, okay. Thanks."

She moaned. "Oh, no."

He looked up. "What?"

"I've already discussed it with my brother," she confessed, grimacing.

Tyler threw up his hands, appalled at his own behavior and apparently powerless to change it. "Well, that's just great!"

A horrible thought occurred, staggering him. Stupid as it seemed, it spoiled so much that he hadn't even realized mattered to him. Unfortunately, though, it made an awful sense. Small towns were even more notorious for gossip than Dallas society. Everyone knew it. Everyone.

"That's why they were all so friendly to me today."

Charlotte blinked, obviously taken aback. "What are you talking about?"

"The whole town must know!" he erupted. "Why else would they fall all over themselves?"

Her jaw dropped, and for some reason that just stoked his temper, that and the secret, niggling knowledge that he'd gone from overreaction to completely unreasonable. It wasn't her fault. She couldn't help who he was or what she knew. How could she know that he'd hoped to remain incognito, so to speak?

"Now, that's just silly," she finally told him, folding her arms. "Folks in Eden are naturally friendly. It has nothing to do with who your family is!"

"How do I know that?" he demanded.

The compassion warming her eyes made him want to run and at the same time to reach for her. In the end, to his everlasting shock, she was the one to reach out, wrapping her slender arms around his shoulders.

"Oh, Tyler."

She placed her bright head on his shoulder, her face turned away from him. His indignation evaporated like so much mist, leaving behind a sheepish sense of foolishness and a deep chasm of pure need.

His hands somehow landed at her waist, tentatively clasping the delicate curves. For several long, sweet moments it felt as if some calming, invisible balm flowed across his savaged nerve endings. Like parched earth soaking up gentle rain, he absorbed the comfort that she so effortlessly offered. How had she known that he needed this when he hadn't known himself?

"I always thought it would be a terrible burden to have too much money and to be known for it," she whispered.

He sighed, confessing, "It is not a simple life, that's for sure."

After several moments, she quietly asked, "Who hurt you so badly that you would be this suspicious of people who just want to be friendly?"

He squeezed his eyes shut. *Who hasn't?* he thought. He said, "When money's involved, you

never know who your real friends are. I'm not sure
you can even have real friends."

She pulled away at that, folding closed the front
of the oversize cardigan that she wore over a simple
plaid shirt, its tail tucked primly into the belted
waistband of slender jeans. "Of course you can.
Not everyone is after your money."

"You wouldn't say that if you'd been around
when my father lay dying," he told her, pushing a
hand through his hair. "Everyone behaved like a
pack of jackals, snarling and snapping over every
nickel and dime of his personal fortune. Contrac-
tors, business associates, even the upper management at our own company...." Tyler shook his head
remembering that even his father's broker had
wrenched every penny from the estate that he could
by freezing his father's accounts and dumping them
into interest-bearing escrow then slapping on every
management fee he could dream up.

"Charities called up begging for final bequests,"
he told her. "Complete strangers accosted me on the
street claiming that my father had promised them
money." He threw up his hands. "The blasted doctor
asked for a grant to do cancer research!"

He went on, telling her the details of those awful
last weeks, the words pouring out of him as if they'd
been too long pent up.

Granted, Comstock Aldrich had been a for-
midable force, and he'd never taken a step without
calculating the return in dollars and cents, but surely

he'd deserved some dignity in death, some consideration of his basic humanity. Instead, everyone around him had turned into vultures, picking over the corpse before he'd even drawn his last breath. It had fallen to Tyler to hold the scavengers at bay.

Her eyes sad, Charlotte listened patiently, murmuring occasional condolences.

"That's how it is when you have real money," Tyler finished glumly.

"I'm not surprised," she admitted softly. "I always imagined it would be like that. I'd rather have Christ, frankly."

Tyler tilted his head. He didn't have the faintest idea what she meant by that. How could anyone *have* Christ? And what did that have to do with anything?

Suddenly he felt out of place, out of sync. With a pang, he realized that he'd done it again, told her much more than he'd ever told anyone.

Shocked, he backed up a step, lifting a hand to the nape of his neck. What was it about this woman that turned him into a babbling lunatic? Gulping, he wasn't even sure that he wanted to know.

"I-I've kept you long enough," he said politely, backing away.

She started as if just coming to herself. "I have to check the oven."

"I have to…" He waved an arm. Do something. Anything. But what?

Already moving away, she lifted a finger. "Could

you hold that thought for a minute? I'll be right back."

Tyler watched her move across the pavement to the kitchen door of the apartment, then stood awkwardly while she went in, the screen slapping closed behind her.

He wanted to flee—and to stay, for some inexplicable reason, except, of course, that he didn't really have anyplace to go or anything to do. And he didn't want to be alone.

For once, Tyler realized with a pang, he really wanted not to be alone.

Chapter Five

Tyler had never known a moment of real want in his lifetime, but he realized that he had somehow always been alone. Even with servants in the house and a mother who had nothing better to do than socialize and shop, he'd spent a great deal of his childhood virtually by himself.

True, he'd basically done as he pleased, and as a boy he'd often preferred to tag along with various friends and their families rather than bicker unsupervised at home with his sister and brother. There had been whole years when he'd probably slept over at a buddy's place as many or more nights as he'd slept at home, and the fact that his family hardly seemed to notice had made him feel rather bereft at times.

Tyler didn't like feeling needy, but he liked even less the idea of spending the evening alone in that shabby little room behind him. Even as he warred with himself, he wandered closer to that kitchen door.

"Sorry, Granddad," he heard Charlotte say.

Hap said something in return, but Tyler couldn't make out the words. It had been a long time since he'd felt so much on the outside looking in. He didn't like it one bit, but he didn't move away.

Charlotte returned a few moments later with a smile on her face. "I don't know why I thought he wouldn't help himself to his own dinner," she said, pulling the door closed behind her and stepping out of the way of the screen. "He is not, as he has reminded me, helpless."

Tyler chuckled and nodded. "I take it that the domino game has adjourned."

"Only so long as it takes them to eat dinner," Charlotte said with a grin. "Justus is in there, helping himself to one of Ryan's pot pies."

"You really do always cook extra for your brothers, don't you?" Tyler said. "Or is it really for them?" He nodded toward the lobby, indicating the inveterate domino players.

She shrugged. "Them or whoever."

It occurred to him that he would have to find his own dinner tonight, and that fact made him feel lonely again. Staring off toward the highway, he pondered just why that might be since he often ate alone.

Before he reached any sort of conclusion, a vaguely familiar, dirty white pickup truck swung off the shoulder of the road and turned into the motel property. The driver did not pull into the drive-through as a motel patron would have done but came to a halt right beside them.

A tall, lean cowboy hung out the window, flipping them a wave. "Hey, sugar! You about ready there? My belly's kissing my backbone."

Tyler remembered now why that truck seemed familiar. He'd seen it there before, just last night in fact. Obviously this cowboy made a habit of stopping by to see Charlotte. Jealousy struck Tyler like a hammer blow. In the same instant he realized how ridiculous he was being.

Of course she would have a boyfriend. The wonder was that she hadn't married already. He remembered something she'd said about the pickings being slim in a small town, but that didn't mean the local male populace wouldn't realize what a gem they had in their midst. They were probably in constant pursuit. If things were different, he might well be himself, not that he had the time and freedom for personal relationships, or the inclination to pursue them. Why bother when so few people could be trusted to look past his fortune? Besides, he had a very demanding job.

His life suddenly seemed rather shallow and truncated. Had distrust completely overtaken him? Why, even his father had found the time and fortitude to get married. Twice. Tyler found himself wondering just what it would take to win Charlotte away from the cowboy.

Belatedly Tyler realized that Charlotte was speaking.

"Knock off work a little earlier," she said with a cheeky grin, addressing the driver of that truck.

Tyler had missed whatever had led up to that point, but he assumed that this was in reference to the cowboy being hungry.

"Look who's talking," the fellow drawled. "Don't tell me you've been standing around here waiting for hours on end."

"We were sitting, actually," Tyler put in, quite without meaning to. "Well, most of the time." Couldn't hurt, he mused, to let the other man know that he might have a little competition.

Charlotte laughed and waved a hand at Tyler. "Holt, this is Tyler Aldrich. He's been keeping me company, and I guess we did kind of let time get away from us. This is my brother Holt."

Her brother. Tyler didn't know whether he felt more relieved or embarrassed, which meant that he wound up being both, not that he let on. Putting out his hand, he stepped closer to the truck.

"Pleased to meet you."

"Likewise."

Holt reached across himself to shake hands, but the gesture contained a certain wariness. Tyler sensed that the eyes hidden in the shadow of that hat brim keenly assessed him. The grip of that calloused hand held a hint of warning, too, as if its owner wanted him to know that force could be brought to bear should it prove necessary.

"Come on, sprite," Holt called to Charlotte. "My dinner's waiting."

She skipped forward, brushing a hand against Tyler's forearm. "Maybe you'd like to join us? I know you haven't eaten, and the café closed at six."

Tyler smiled to himself. That was one problem solved.

"But be warned," she cautioned, "we're headed to the catfish joint."

"What's wrong with catfish?" Holt wanted to know. "We eat catfish every Saturday night."

"You eat catfish every Saturday night," she corrected. By way of explanation, she added to Tyler, "Holt takes either me or Granddad to dinner every Saturday night."

"Sometimes both of you," Holt put in.

"But not often," she clarified. "Someone usually has to stay here in case a guest drops in. It's my turn to go out this week."

"I see."

"You might as well come," she prodded. "It's either the Watermelon Patch, the truck stop up in Waurika or driving an hour or so to find another restaurant."

Tyler smiled, his decision made from the moment she'd issued the invitation. "I'd like to come along. Thank you."

Beaming, she hurried around the front end of the truck to the passenger door, Tyler following on her heels.

"After all," he said, reaching around to open the door for her, "I have to eat. Might as well do it in good company."

Perhaps the food wouldn't be particularly healthy, but no matter, and he didn't care what the tall cowboy behind the steering wheel might have to say about it. Charlotte's pleased smile gave him all the encouragement he needed, and then some.

Charlotte could not quite believe her own audacity. Imagine a man like Tyler Aldrich at a hole-in-the-wall like the Watermelon Patch. Then again, he'd rented a room in her motel and would apparently be staying a second night. She mentally shook her head. Slumming, perhaps? Or could he be as lonely as he seemed?

God knew that she wouldn't be in his shoes for anything in this world. Money like Tyler seemed to possess could only be a burden. He'd said so himself. At least she knew that her friends and family loved her for herself. She looked over at Holt, her fingertips brushing his shoulders fondly. He seemed to take that as a cue, lifting his gaze to the rearview mirror and the man in the backseat.

"Aldrich, huh? Charlotte says you're connected with the grocery stores. That so?"

She heard Tyler shift on the cloth seat. "Yeah,

that's right. It so happens I'm CEO of Aldrich &
Associates."

Holt let out a thin whistle, thin enough to let Tyler
know that he wasn't too impressed. She cut her eyes
at her brother, tempted to pinch him. What was
wrong with him? Holt never behaved rudely.
Perhaps he didn't trust as easily as Ryan and
Granddad, but he could always be counted on to be
friendly and fair, except...

She widened her eyes, remembering another time
when Holt had been less than cordial, less than welcoming. He took his position as big brother to heart,
and he'd never quite trusted her one serious boyfriend. To this day, Holt seemed to suspect that Jerry
had broken her heart, rather than the other way
around.

The implications shook her. Surely, Holt did not
consider Tyler Aldrich to be a romantic prospect.
The man lived in Dallas! He was passing through
Eden, nothing more. Scoffing at the very idea, she
fixed her big brother with a stern, wide-eyed stare.

He jerked his head at her, as if asking what he
could possibly be indicted for, but she looked at him
until he sighed and slumped in his seat. Smiling to
herself, she turned her gaze out the window.

The rest of the drive passed in silence.

The Watermelon Patch restaurant proved to be
something of a revelation for Tyler. For one thing,
it sat smack dab in the middle of a real, honest-to-

goodness watermelon field, though Tyler wouldn't have known that if Charlotte hadn't told him. In the dark, it looked pretty much like any empty field to him, but then he knew little about watermelons beyond when they were in season and the mark-up per unit. The building itself claimed most of his interest, though.

Cobbled together of sheet metal and weathered wood, mismatched windows, a variety of shingle types in several different colors and—amazingly— a sliding-glass door that appeared to have been salvaged from a burned-out house, the structure would not have passed any legal standard anywhere in the United States of America.

Oily smoke chugged from a leaning stack pipe on one end of the building, smudging the night sky with dirty gray and blanketing the whole area with the aromas of frying foods, while specks of light and a virtual cacophony of voices spilled out of the chinks and cracks in the walls. The whole thing looked as if it might tumble down should an errant breeze come its way.

Despite the restaurant's decrepit appearance, the joint seemed to literally jump with the movement of bodies packed inside. Automobiles of every description crowded the sandy parking area, but Holt didn't let that deter him as he angled the tall, long truck into a narrow space between a tree at the edge of the road and a massive propane tank. The tree stood so close to the passenger side of the truck that both Tyler and Charlotte had to slide across the cab to exit on the driver's side, Charlotte from the front seat, Tyler from the back.

He saw at once that he hadn't underestimated Holt's height. Tyler stood a solid six feet in his socks, but Holt had at least three inches on him, and that did not count the heels of his boots or the tall crown on that cowboy hat. Tyler doubted very much that had anything to do with why Holt removed the hat, revealing a handsome head of thick, sandy-brown hair and vibrant green eyes.

"Looks like another full house," he said, placing the hat, brim up, on the truck seat before closing and locking the door.

"Come Saturday night, you can't even find an empty chair to lay a hat on in there," Charlotte explained to Tyler.

Looping a brotherly arm around Charlotte's shoulders, Holt walked her toward the restaurant, leaving Tyler to trail along behind them. He did not think it unintentional. Wondering how long they'd have to wait before a table opened, he kept up.

In the restaurants that he normally frequented, Tyler didn't do much waiting, but he didn't mind the idea of cooling his heels a bit just now, provided he didn't do it standing alone in some dingy corner while Holt chatted up Charlotte across the room. He wouldn't put that little maneuver past Charlotte's brother, which partly amused Tyler and partly irritated him. Usually, the family members of young women cultivated his interest rather than shunned it. Perhaps that accounted for his general lack of interest.

To Tyler's surprise, they did not wait at all. Instead, a plump, fortyish, ponytailed, bleach-blond, gap-toothed waitress led them through a rabbit's warren of tables and chairs, across uneven floors, to a short bench against the back wall. Charlotte and Holt took seats on the bench. The waitress—Joanie, Tyler thought he heard her called—then shoved a narrow plank table in front of them, jostling several other patrons in the process. Next she plunked down sets of flatware tightly wrapped in paper napkins. Finally, she dragged over a chair for Tyler, its wooden legs bound up with wire to keep them from spreading.

He'd barely lowered himself onto the scarred seat when Joanie produced a pencil and pad, asking, "So what'll you folks have this evening?"

Tyler glanced around. "I, um, seem to have missed the menu."

"Oh, there's no menu, sugar," Joanie told him, cracking the chewing gum tucked into her cheek. "There's just catfish, taters, beans and slaw. All I need to know is how many pieces you want."

"Pieces?" He looked to Charlotte for clarification.

"Of fish."

"I'll have four," Holt announced decisively.

"Two," Charlotte said when Joanie looked to her.

The waitress turned her heavily lined eyes on Tyler. He picked a number for sheer symmetry's sake.

"Put me in between with three, I guess."

"How do you want those potatoes?"

"Fried," Holt answered.

"Baked," Tyler said at the same time.

They looked at each other, then away.

"None for me, thanks," Charlotte said.

"You want that spud loaded?" Joanie asked.

"Sour cream only. Fat-free, if you've got it." She gave him a bland look over the top of her pad. "Never mind."

"I'll bring y'all's tea and cornbread in a minute." She danced off, twisting and turning and smacking her gum.

Other diners shifted around in their chairs to greet the Jeffords, reaching across one another to shake hands with Tyler as Holt gave them his name. Conversation engulfed them.

"You find a buyer for that old rig yet, Holt?"

"Not looking."

"I hear Sharp's lease has expired."

Holt just shook his head at that.

"Hap keeping Ryan in line tonight, I guess."

"He's got some school deal tonight," Charlotte answered.

"More like the other way around, anyhow," Holt put in, and laughter followed.

"Did you hear that Jenny Tumm's old mother

passed?" someone asked from across the room. "Died in her sleep, they say."

"She must've been a hundred," someone else observed.

"Ninety-seven," another voice contended. "I'll tell you how I know."

A recitation of names, dates and weather patterns followed, devolving quickly into various reminiscences about droughts and deluges survived, tornadoes succumbed to and a horribly late frost that had prodded the proprietor to hedge his bets with a restaurant in case his melons failed to make it again. Weather, it turned out, held a prominent place in the local, agriculture-based psyche.

Tyler listened unabashedly, caught up in the feel of community that must be particular to small-town life. Like a large family dinner, everyone talked over one another while they ate, but no one shouted in anger as often happened on those rare occasions when the Aldrich brood sat down together.

Charlotte's eye would catch his from time to time, and a small, knowing smile would curve her lovely lips, as if she saw how fascinating and foreign he found all this. He didn't try to hide his interest, only to retain a polite dignity, and to let her know that he enjoyed himself. He couldn't, in fact, recall an occasion when he'd enjoyed himself more.

Joanie returned to plunk down plastic baskets of steaming cornbread squares and tall jars of iced tea, accompanied by a bowl of sugar, another of lemon wedges and a third piled high with butter spooned out of a tub. With the possibility of bread plates dim at best, Tyler followed Holt's lead and reached for a square of that high, light, mouth-watering cornbread, his belly suddenly growling.

The bread burned his hand, but the aroma wouldn't let him put it down. Breaking off pieces with his fingertips, he poked them into his mouth, and closed his eyes as they seemed to melt on his tongue. Holt, meanwhile, slathered his piece with enough butter to guarantee a heart attack in a less fit man and scarfed it down in a single bite. He then proceeded to stir half a cup of sugar into his already sweet tea and suck the glass dry, while Charlotte looked on. Tyler held off as long as he could on a second piece of cornbread, straining his vaunted control.

Ever since his seemingly healthy father had been diagnosed with cancer, Tyler had tried to live with an eye to his own body's well-being. He'd developed an exercise routine, with the help of a private trainer, and consulted a dietitian on food choice and preparation. He'd hired a chef trained to produce whole-grain, low-fat, well-balanced dishes on a Mediterranean model with Asian influences, and routinely chose restaurants based on their ability to accommodate his preferences.

He'd limited caffeine, forsworn all but the most moderate amounts of alcohol, avoided secondhand smoke and cut out sugar and white flour. In truth, he hadn't missed a single item that he'd given up. But then he'd never eaten cornbread so sweet and soft and buttery that it all but fell apart on its way to his watering mouth or tea so fragrant and smooth that it begged to slide down his throat.

He'd already tossed prudence to the wind by the time Joanie brought a second basket of what Charlotte referred to as "corncake" to the table along with paper-lined baskets of golden fish fillets heaped atop thick slices of crisp fries, or in his case, crowded around a steaming potato the size of a football. This came accompanied with generous bowls of red beans and coleslaw and cups of creamy tartar sauce. Tyler managed to resist only the latter. The rest of it remained untouched only so long as it took Holt to pray over it.

Tyler tried not to appear uneasy when brother and sister joined hands and bowed their heads over the rough table. He might have succeeded if the whole place hadn't gone suddenly quiet, allowing Holt's voice to carry.

"Heavenly Father, we thank You for Your bounty and seek Your blessing on this food and all those within the confines of this building. Keep us mindful of Your love and grace. We pray in the name of Your Son. Amen."

"Amens" wafted around the building. Tyler shifted, feeling uncertain. These Jeffords were sure praying people. Praying at the dinner table in the privacy of one's home was one thing, but he'd never seen anyone pray in such a public setting before. Here, however, it seemed perfectly acceptable.

Knives and forks clinked, someone laughed and conversation resumed, quickly growing to previous decibels. Holt attacked his food like a man starved.

Tyler tried to display more control, cringing a little at the grease glistening on the crispy coating of the fish. He flaked some of the breading off with his fork, but in the end he ate every piece and wished he'd ordered more. The potato, baked to perfection and heaped with sour cream, filled his mouth with warm, hearty delight. He quickly filled up, but still managed to taste the beans and slaw.

At least he intended only to taste the slaw. Surprised by the fresh flavor of the shredded cabbage and other vegetables, he ate all of the coleslaw despite the calorie-rich dressing. Only later did he reflect that the meaty, tasty beans probably comprised the most healthy part of the whole meal, but he simply didn't have room for more than a few bites.

Charlotte ate steadily, but after Holt polished off what he'd been served, he finished her portion and sat eyeing what Tyler had left over until Joanie returned with dishes of peach cobbler swimming in cream. Too full even to be tempted, Tyler shoved his dessert across the table and watched it disappear beneath Holt's spoon while Charlotte made a fair dent in hers.

Sighing with satisfaction, Holt at last sat back,

stretched out his long legs and crossed his ankles, his heels on the floor next to Tyler's chair. "Now that's what I call eating."

Tyler laughed. "I'd hate to see what you call pigging out."

"I'm a hardworking man," Holt said with mock defensiveness, his green gaze settling on Tyler. "What is it exactly that a CEO does?"

Tyler knew when he was being measured, and he also knew that a man like Holt wouldn't be impressed with mere position. He wouldn't demean himself by trying to convince Charlotte's brother that he did more than delegate. "A great deal."

"I'll bet," Holt said. Not a hint of disdain had colored Holt's voice, but neither did it contain even the barest inflection of admiration.

"I'm sure it's a huge job," Charlotte said quickly.

Warmed by her defense of him, Tyler just smiled. Tyler could feel another question hovering in the air, but he would not prompt it. Instead, he simply waited.

After a moment, a slight smile twisted one corner of Holt's mouth, but he did not disappoint. "So what's an important CEO doing in our little Eden?"

Tyler smiled to himself. "Just passing through."

"Don't take more'n a minute to just pass through," Holt pointed out.

Tyler propped his forearms against the tabletop. "Just biding my time, then."

"In Eden," Holt said doubtfully.

Tyler considered, but why dither? If pressed,

Charlotte would undoubtedly repeat what he'd told her earlier. Why shouldn't she? "All right," he said. "If you must know, I'm hiding."

Holt sat forward abruptly, bracing his elbows on the table top. "From who?"

"From people who aggravate me."

"Is that a long list?"

"Long enough."

"But hopefully not growing," Charlotte said anxiously.

He chuckled. "Not lately."

Holt relaxed a bit, asking, "How long you plan on hiding out around here?"

"Oh, I don't know," Tyler answered, surprising himself. "A while yet."

"Well, you might as well come along to church tomorrow, then," Holt said.

The invitation sounded off-hand and casual, but Tyler knew better than that. He knew a challenge when he heard one. He knew, too, that he'd gain this man's respect only by attending church with the family the next day. Surprisingly, he found that he wanted this man's respect. That being the case, the decision seemed simple.

"Might as well. Nothing else to do, except sleep, and there's all afternoon for that."

Holt reached past Tyler, and when he drew back his hand, he had the dinner tab tucked between two fingers. Tyler automatically reached for his wallet, but Holt waved him off.

"Naw, now, that wouldn't be neighborly."

Neighborly, as they both knew, had nothing to do with it. "At least let me pay my share," Tyler insisted.

"Not this time."

Bemused, Tyler tilted his head. "Can't I at least leave a tip?"

"You better," Joanie said from behind him, and everyone around laughed, including Holt.

Tyler had a twenty out of his pocket in a flash. Holding it up, he tilted back his head, asking, "Will this do?"

She snatched that twenty so fast her hand blurred. More laughter followed, including Tyler's own. Then a grinning Charlotte rose in the small space at the end of the bench.

Tyler rose and stepped away, allowing Holt to push back the table. Charlotte slipped around her end and came to Tyler's side. His hand moved of its own volition to the small of her back as they turned toward the exit, and it stayed there until they stepped out of the building. Holt remained inside to pay the bill at the narrow counter set up in one corner near the door.

Tyler stood in the darkness next to Charlotte, feeling sated and happy and restful. "Thank you for inviting me to join you."

"Glad you did," she said, folding her arms.

"Me, too."

He hunched his shoulders against the chill and

debated the wisdom of slipping his arms around her. Holt spared him the decision by sliding back the glass door just then and stepping outside. Tyler put down his head and turned toward the truck, pleased that Charlotte stayed at his side.

Only as Holt paused at the open truck, fitting that cowboy hat onto his head once more, did Tyler fully realize what he'd done by accepting an invitation to attend church. What on earth was he going to wear?

Chapter Six

Standing next to Tyler on the pavement at the motel, Charlotte watched her brother's long legs stride toward the building. Tyler spoke to Holt as he opened the screen on the kitchen door.

"Thanks again for dinner."

Holt waved a hand negligently. "No problem. See you in the morning." He paused and looked back over his shoulder. "Provided you don't change your mind."

Charlotte sighed inwardly. What was wrong with him? Did he have to make even an invitation to church sound like a challenge?

"I won't change my mind," Tyler replied evenly. She tried not to be too pleased by that. Tyler or anyone else attending church was a good thing, but it didn't have anything to do with her personally.

"You coming in?" Holt asked Charlotte. Her brother usually stopped in after dinner to speak to Hap.

"In a minute." She felt that she owed Tyler a private word. Holt had needled him all evening, and she didn't want Tyler to get the wrong impression. Holt split a look between her and Tyler, then went through the door shaking his head.

Charlotte glanced at Tyler, not quite sure what to say. "I hope you weren't offended by Holt's behavior this evening."

"Offended? Why would I be offended? Guys prod each other all the time."

He actually sounded pleased. She breathed a silent sigh of relief. "I just didn't want you to think it's because of who you are or anything."

Grinning ear-to-ear, Tyler rocked back on his heels. "Yeah, I know. Anyone hanging around his little sister would get the same treatment."

She blinked, then laughed. "True. It's nothing personal."

"Oh, it's personal," Tyler said. "Your brother wants to protect you. I can only respect that."

She sighed, saying, "I don't need protecting. I'm not seventeen, I'm twenty-seven."

Tyler's pale eyes seemed to glow. "True. For the record, I'm glad I went along. I really enjoyed myself. Thanks for inviting me."

"I'm glad, too."

"I, um, I do have a problem, though," Tyler said, rubbing his chin, "and I'm going to need some help with it."

Charlotte jerked a little straighter. "Oh?"

He held out the sides of his suit coat, saying, "I'm standing here in the only clothes I have, and I've been standing in them quite long enough. I need to come up with something for tomorrow. So what do folks wear to church around here and where can I get that?"

Charlotte hadn't even thought of such a dilemma, but obviously he was right. The man needed a change of clothes. She could try washing things for him, but she'd prefer not even to touch such obviously expensive articles. What if she ruined something? Still, she'd help if she could. Christian charity demanded it, regardless of his social status.

She eyed him critically for a moment, then shook her head. "I'm sure my brothers would lend you something, but Ryan's too wide and Holt's too tall. And Granddad—" she waved a hand dismissively "—his wardrobe's straight out of the 1950s."

Tyler seemed genuinely distressed. She imagined that image was very important to a man in his position, which must only enhance his need.

"What am I going to do? I don't even know what I should be wearing. I mean, at home, I always wear a suit and tie when I go to church."

Her ears perked up at that, glad to hear that he went to church back in Dallas. She wondered if he was a regular attender, then pushed the thought aside in order to tackle the more immediate issue.

"Suit and tie are fine, of course."

"But this suit needs dry cleaning," he pointed out. "Not even a good pressing will do at this point. I can manage the tie, but that's about it."

She tapped her foot, thinking. He could beg off, but it was *church.* He should go. She wanted him to go. For his own good, of course.

Oh, all right, it was more than that. In all truth, she liked him. A great deal. She hadn't wanted to drive away and leave him here alone tonight, and she wanted him to go to church with the family in the morning. So what if he would be gone before sunset tomorrow? That was just as it should be, but he still had a problem.

For the man to attend church he had to have clean clothes, and she couldn't blame him for not wanting to wear that suit for a third day.

Charlotte glanced at Tyler and found him gazing down at her patiently. "Okay," she said, embracing the project. "Let's look at our options."

"What would those options be?"

Sucking in a deep breath, she considered. "I could always wash whatever is washable."

"And I would still be stuck wearing a dirty suit," he pointed out.

"Exactly. Guess that means driving to Duncan."

Even if they'd realized earlier in the day that clothing for him would be an issue, Duncan would have been the only option. Women's clothing could be found in Eden, but not men's.

"Duncan," he mused. "How far is that?"

"About thirty-five miles."

"Ah." He looked off in that direction as if he might actually catch sight of the place. "They have a mall in Duncan, do they?"

"Uh, sure. Sort of. But all the stores in the mall will be closing…" she looked at her watch "…right about now."

"Oh." He grimaced. "Plan C, then, I guess, huh? Please say you have a Plan C."

She shook her head. "Nope. Plan B was and is to drive up to the twenty-four-hour discount store in Duncan. That's not part of the mall."

"Discount store?" he parroted doubtfully.

"You won't find anything else open at this time of night," she told him. "Not around here."

Glancing at his wrist, he smiled wryly. "You wouldn't in Dallas, either."

"Well, there you go."

He leaned forward. "There *we* go. I hope." Ducking his head, he looked up at her from beneath the crag of his brow and admitted sheepishly, "To tell you the truth, I've never done much shopping."

She rolled her eyes, half convinced that he was joking. "Oh, please. A man with your money—"

"Can hire someone else to shop for him," he interrupted flatly, averting his gaze. "I shop for investments, big-ticket items like cars and boats and property, and even then someone else has done the research for me. When it comes to clothes, I get fittings and pick out fabrics. From a grouping which my fashion consultant has already decided are appropriate."

Charlotte must have stood there with her mouth open for a full minute or more before she realized that she was gaping. Hastily she cleared her throat. "Right. Okay. I'll, um, just let Granddad know where I'll be."

Tyler heaved a great sigh of relief. "Thank you. Again. I'll get the car." He slid his hand into the pocket of his pants. "Meet you right here."

"Five minutes," she promised as they parted.

She found Hap sitting at the dining room table with Holt. As usual, Holt somehow managed to sprawl his long body over the chair without winding up on the floor. For such a hardworking man, he could look as lazy and boneless as an old hound dog, but he always said his energy all went to his brain cells at times like this. She didn't doubt it.

Charlotte bent and pressed her cheek to her grandfather's forehead. "How're you feeling?"

"Oh, I'm fine, darlin'. Don't you go worrying about me." His merry eyes twinkled. "Holt says y'all took Tyler Aldrich to dinner with you."

She glanced at her brother. "So we did. He seemed to enjoy himself."

Hap's bushy white eyebrows moved upward. "Enough to accept an invitation to church tomorrow, I hear."

Nodding, she said, "Yeah, there's a little problem with that, though, so I need to go out again for a while. Do you mind staying up until I get back?"

He twisted slightly in his chair. "Where're you going, hon?"

She could feel Holt's gaze drilling into her, and she knew what he thought, that her interest in Tyler was personal, but as she'd said earlier, she wasn't seventeen anymore. She knew her own mind, and she had a clear vision of her life and world. Tyler had no place in that world, other than a very temporary one.

"Tyler has nothing clean to wear to church tomorrow, so I'm going to help him find something at the discount store in Duncan."

"Ah." Hap grinned so wide that his dentures clacked, but he quickly shuttered his expression, glancing at Holt. Obviously they'd been discussing her and Tyler, and just as obviously Holt had made his opinion known. She wondered what he found so objectionable about Tyler, but then she reminded herself that it didn't matter. He and Hap were both wrong if they thought anything would or could come from what was, essentially, an act of Christian charity on her part.

"He can't buy his own clothes?" Holt asked sardonically.

She folded her arms, getting to the real issue. "There is no reason I shouldn't help him out."

"That's exactly right," Hap said, repositioning in his chair again. "Y'all be careful, hon. I'll take care of the desk. I'm going to be up a couple more hours anyhow."

"I'll help you," Holt added in a flat tone.

"You will get yourself home and to bed," Hap replied good-naturedly, pointing a gnarled finger at Holt. He flicked that same finger between himself and Charlotte. "Neither of us need sitting up for."

"You like him," Holt accused, narrowing his eyes at Hap. "You just want to give her a chance to start something with Mr. Big Bucks out there."

"Well, what of it?" Hap retorted, not even bothering to deny it. "She deserves a good man, and they don't exactly hang off the trees around here."

Exasperated at the way the men in her life seemed to be jumping to all sorts of unwarranted conclusions, Charlotte threw up her hands. "You're both being ridiculous," she scolded lightly, marching around the table to drop a kiss on her brother's head. "I'm not starting anything with anyone." She moved on to Hap, repeating the process with him. "And if I was, it wouldn't be with him."

"Why not?" Hap demanded. "I do like that boy. He's not such a big shot he can't rub elbows with the little people."

"Granted, but he's a big shot who lives and works in Dallas," she reminded them, figuring that said it all.

They both knew perfectly well that she'd broken off her engagement when her fiancé, Jerry, had insisted that he couldn't make a decent living around Eden, and she'd known Jerry Moody her whole life. They'd dated for years before getting engaged, but she hadn't wanted to trade her small-town life for the big city then, and she still didn't.

Holt smiled, but she couldn't tell whether she saw relief there or something else. It simply did not matter. Not at all.

She went out without another word, ignoring the little voice in her head that whispered Tyler Aldrich, a grown man who ran a huge corporation, could surely buy his own clothes without assistance from her, had he wanted to. And provided she had been of a mind to let him.

Charlotte tried not to be impressed as she sank into the luxurious leather seat. If dinner had somehow blurred the differences between them, then this extravagant automobile served to under-score them, especially when Tyler tapped the screen of the in-dash computer. She watched as he chose a destination from those listed, state first and then city, before he turned to her.

"Address?"

"I beg your pardon?"

"The discount store, do you know the address?"

"Uh, no, actually I don't."

"How about an intersection? Anything near will work."

She racked her brain for a moment, then gave the only street name she could remember. "81 and Elder."

He chuckled. "What is it with you Oklahomans

and trees? Half the streets in this state seem to be named for trees."

Charlotte shrugged, smiling. "Never thought about it."

The computer did its thing, a flashing light indicating the exact location of the discount store.

"I thought I was supposed to show you where it is," she said, wondering again why she'd agreed to this, given the suppositions of her family and the fact that he could obviously find his way around without her.

"You know that's not the only reason I asked for your help," he told her, guiding the car out onto the highway.

"Uh-huh. You don't know how to shop."

He shot her a look, smiled and said, "I've got to confess something."

She sat up a little straighter, her heart suddenly pounding. "What?"

"I've never been in a discount store in my life."

She shook her head, feeling oddly deflated. What had she expected? "It's not like you have to have a membership to get in the door or anything."

"I know that. What I don't know is what I should be looking for or where I should be looking for it. Those stores are huge. I told you, I'm used to someone else narrowing down my choices. Then I just stand there and let the tailor measure me. Even then, he usually comes to me."

"I see." She'd known people lived like that, of

course—in some other universe. "Talk about your worlds colliding," she muttered under her breath.

"What's that?"

"Nothing. Nothing at all." Which was exactly what would come of this little exercise in Christian charity, no matter what Hap might hope.

She knew the foolishness of even entertaining the possibility of getting involved with this man. Hap might think him grand, and perhaps he was, but surely everyone saw how ill-suited the two of them really were. She didn't want any part of his world, and she didn't want to be the woman that he saw whenever he decided to amuse himself by going slumming. That being the case, this little adventure could be nothing more than that. Period. In fact, she couldn't imagine why she wasted her time and energy even thinking about it. So she would stop, with a little help.

"Father," she prayed silently, *"You know I only want to do Your will, and I know that You mean for me to stay in Eden. Granddad and the boys need me, and I need them. You showed me when Jerry had to leave Eden that my place is here with my family. Don't let me be distracted by worldly things or tempted into building dreams and hopes that just aren't part of Your plan for me. Amen."*

Feeling a bit better, she settled back to enjoy the ride, and what a ride it was. They flew. At least it felt like they did, the car skimming over the ground with smooth, leashed power. Charlotte found it thrilling, but she didn't want to think about how fast they were traveling, not that she could help doing so when the computer displayed their speed in numbers two-inches high.

Seeing her unease, Tyler backed off. "Sorry. I let this thing get away from me sometimes."

She smiled her thanks for his consideration and felt comfortable enough to mention minutes later that they were approaching a known speed trap in the community ahead. He backed off a little more, and the remainder of the journey passed in companionable silence. Almost before she knew it, they hit the 81 bypass that skirted the downtown area of Duncan.

A community of some twenty-five thousand souls, Duncan provided the major shopping for Stephens county and large portions of the counties surrounding it. Still, area residents thought nothing of traveling to Lawton, Oklahoma City, Wichita Falls or even Dallas for major purchases.

Tyler parked the sports car in a remote section of a parking lot crowded with automobiles. "Hope you don't mind walking a bit," he said. "After that meal, I could use a little exercise, and I don't like to park this baby too close to others."

"No problem."

She didn't wait for him to come around the car and open the door for her, meeting him at the rear of the vehicle instead. He set the locks remotely and fell into step beside her, his hand hovering at the small of her back as it had earlier at the restaurant that evening.

That small gesture both tickled and troubled her. It had been a long time since a man had acted with any measure of gallantry toward her. On the other hand, this was not, after all, a date. She'd dated so little in the past several years that she had almost forgotten what it felt like to have a man behave with a touch of chivalry. That's all this was, though. Nothing more. It certainly was not a romance.

Despite what her grandfather seemed to believe, Charlotte had come to suspect that God did not mean for her life to include romance, even if she sometimes secretly grieved the loss of such dreams as marriage and children of her own. She knew perfectly well that God, being the God of miracles, could yet work out those things for her, but she considered herself a realist. What she'd told Tyler earlier about the pickings being slim around Eden was the perfect truth.

All the men in her age range were either already married or had moved away. Moreover, nice, upstanding single men just did not pull out a map and decide they were going to build their lives in Eden, Oklahoma. No one ever moved into Eden unless they already had a connection there, so she couldn't expect to meet her true love walking down the street one day.

No, she was not meant for romance and marriage—she loved the life she already led. Even the work satisfied her in a very real way. Like Hap, she considered it a ministry, a way to reach out to those in need of a welcoming smile and a safe, comfortable place to lay their heads.

Yes, her life was good. Hap needed her. Her family needed her, and her work mattered. That was enough, more than most people could say about their own lives. In many ways, she mused, she was richer than even Tyler, given what he'd told her that afternoon.

As they entered the store, Tyler would have walked right past the shopping carts if she hadn't stopped to pull one out.

"You'd think I'd have gotten that one right, anyway," he muttered from the corner of his mouth as she pushed the cart down the broad aisle. "We spend a fortune on shopping carts for Aldrich stores."

He came to a stop just past the checkout lanes and looked around in puzzlement. "This is not like any store layout I'm used to. How do you ever find anything in this place?"

"It's not too difficult," she told him. "If you've been in one of these stores you've pretty much been in them all." He frowned down at her, making her dip her head. "Oh, right. You haven't been in one of these stores before."

"Not even to check the grocery prices," he said, glaring at the shelves of goods in the food section. "We have a division that keeps up with that sort of thing, though."

"A whole division? For checking the grocery prices of your competitors?"

"It's a small division," he said a tad defensively.

She strangled an unladylike snort of laughter, coughing into her hand to cover it before steering him toward the men's department. He followed her to a rack of dress slacks, looking around him like he'd never before realized where clothing came from.

Turning a tag over in his hand, he read the price and lifted an eyebrow. "I don't know whether this stuff is dirt cheap or just very poor quality."

"Sometimes both," she said before recommending a certain label. "I find these hold up better after repeated washings."

"Really? You can wash this stuff?" he asked, taking a hanger from the rack and looking over the pants.

She rolled her eyes at him before returning her attention to the selection of dress slacks. "Not everyone drops their clothes at the cleaners. What size do you wear?"

Several seconds passed before she realized that no answer would be forthcoming. She looked around to find him standing with his head bent as if in contemplation, a hand cupping the back of his neck.

"You don't know what size pants you wear?" It came out as much a statement of amazement as a question.

"I'm thinking," he said defensively. "I'm pretty sure the tailor measured me at a thirty-two. Could be thirty-four. Or was it thirty-six?"

"You could always check the label in your slacks," she suggested helpfully, getting a scowl for her efforts.

"Handmade suits don't have size labels," he informed her.

She looked away at that, hiding the lift of her eyebrows. The man was a complete alien. Undoubtedly his whole wardrobe had been handmade to fit, right down to his socks.

"You'll just have to try on several pairs," she decided, selecting a pair and holding them at his waist to judge the length. That pair went back to the rack as she reached for another. "Start in the middle with the thirty-four. We can do down or up from there as we need to."

After several trips to the changing room, he finally settled for chocolate-brown pants that were slightly larger and longer than he'd have liked, but he muttered about not having time to leave them for alteration. Charlotte bit her lip to keep from laughing.

"There is no tailor. They don't do alterations at discount stores."

"Well, how do people get the proper fit?" he asked, sounding exasperated.

"Usually they just wear them as they come."

He frowned at that and put the pants in the shopping cart.

If the slacks were a revelation for him, the shirts were a definite irritant. He turned up his nose at fabrics, styles, patterns, even buttonholes.

"I can't wear these!" he declared, dropping a sleeve in disgust.

"Oh, really?" she said mildly, parking her hands at her waist. "All the other men at church will be wearing them or something very much like them."

Color stained the ridges of his cheekbones. She hadn't meant to embarrass him, but the exchange certainly pointed up the differences between their worlds. Ignoring the white shirts, which he considered too thin, he muttered that he didn't see anything that would go with his tie.

"You can get by without a tie," she told him gently. "Some of the men around here don't even own one."

He looked at her like she must have lost her mind, but he finally opted for a pale blue shirt very near the color of his eyes. Crisis diverted, they moved on to the next item on his agenda, but Charlotte couldn't help whispering a short prayer in her mind.

Thanks, Lord, for showing me how right I am to think that this man and I have nothing whatsoever in common. She just wished the thought didn't sadden her.

Chapter Seven

After some discussion about the necessity of a coat and keeping warm, Tyler chose a nubby brown-and-gray jacket with just a fleck of orange in the tweed. The fit obviously did not please him, but he appeared somewhat mollified when Charlotte complimented him on his sense of color and style.

"Granddad and Holt couldn't put together complimentary colors if they only had two choices."

He chuckled at that, eyes dancing. "Is there a wrong color to go with blue jeans?"

"Point taken."

"Speaking of jeans," he said, craning his neck. "They're a lot more comfortable than dress clothes. Wouldn't hurt if I picked up some."

"Behind the dressing rooms."

"Ah." He headed that way, then stood scratching his ear at the shelves of folded denim. He ran a finger along one shelf. "Boot cut, boot cut, boot cut.

Relaxed boot cut. Regular fit. Relaxed regular. Carpenter." He looked at her with a blatant question in his eyes.

Knowing that he must usually buy according to the designer label and current fashion—as dictated by his fashion consultant, no doubt—she stepped forward to describe the different offerings as well as she could.

"Holt wears these. Snug at the hip and thigh, wider below the knees to accommodate the tops of his boots. It's what the cowboys prefer." She moved along. "Now, Ryan wears these." She held up a pair of the relaxed style. "All the high school girls think he'd look better in the ones that Holt wears, which is why he doesn't wear them. These are still wide enough at the bottom for boots but not so snug up top." She unfolded the next pair so he could see the narrow bottoms. "These are for the left-behinds."

"Left-behinds?"

"You know, those guys left behind in the 1980s when pant legs were just wide enough to get your feet through the openings."

Tyler laughed. She folded the jeans and put them away, teasing as she did so. "You could always wear overalls like Hap."

"Uh, no."

"Then these are probably your best bet," she told him, pulling the right waist size from a stack of regular relaxed fits. He took them without a word, and while he went to try them on, she scoped out the casual knits, thinking the guy must feel like he'd wandered into an alternate universe. In a way, he had.

She shook her head, thinking about the kind of life that didn't even allow for basic shopping. As lost as he seemed to be in her world, though, she knew that she would be much more disoriented in his. The very thought gave her the willies, frankly, and she chafed at sudden gooseflesh on her upper arms.

He returned with the jeans and, to her surprise, went for three pairs, along with several polos and a Henley shirt before taking himself off to pick out socks and a package of undershorts. Evidently she'd miscalculated when she'd assumed that he would be gone by the next evening. She wondered just how long he planned to stay, but she would not ask. She had displayed quite enough unwilling interest already.

With him in control of the shopping cart now, she followed along as he browsed up and down the aisles, taking in everything from kitchenware to television sets. He spent half an hour looking at movies on DVD, and several wound up in his cart. The next thing she knew, he was looking at DVD players. She couldn't keep the questions behind her teeth this time.

"Just happen to need a new DVD player, do you?"

"Actually I thought I'd hook it up in my room back at the motel, if you don't mind."

The motel furnished only TVs with a basic satellite package of some eleven channels.

"I don't mind. You're planning to stay on for a while, are you?" She bit her lip, too late to prevent the one question she'd just decided not to ask.

"A while." He stopped reading the box long enough to look her squarely in the eye. "Is that okay with you?"

"Just fine." She tried to make it sound light and unconcerned, but her voice croaked, trapping her breath in her throat.

He went back to reading the package, a smile playing about his mouth. She worried suddenly that she might be leading him on but the next instant rebuffed that idea.

Who was she kidding? Tyler Aldrich had no more interest in her personally than he did in that DVD player. He was biding his time here, nothing more. He'd admitted it to Holt. Hiding, he'd said, from people who irritated him. Her grandfather's misguided notions had her thinking that Tyler might be staying for another reason, which was clearly beyond ludicrous.

She felt relieved by that realization. Sort of. Except for a kind of amorphous sense of disappointment. Troubled, she knew she would be asking God about that in private later.

Tyler stared at the few remaining bills in his wallet, looked to the readout on the cash register display again, and reached into the pocket of his pants for his money clip. Just the weight of the folded bills within the gold clip told him that he wouldn't have enough to pay for his purchases. The thought of visiting an ATM hadn't even occurred to him. His secretary usually had a certain amount of cash delivered to him every Friday afternoon, but he hadn't been around for that delivery this particular Friday past.

Perhaps he had gone a little overboard with his purchases tonight, but he'd found the experience of shopping so novel that he'd gotten a bit carried away. Just as he'd told Charlotte, he rarely found it necessary to shop and never like this. He usually just had whatever he needed ordered and delivered.

Reluctantly, Tyler opened his wallet to retrieve a credit card. He grimaced, remembering that he carried only his company card. His personal cards remained in the wall safe back at the penthouse. He hadn't given them a thought until this very moment, his routine being to retrieve them, like an expensive personal accessory, only as he dressed to go out for a rare, purely social occasion. That bit of prudence could well prove folly, but nothing could be done about it now. He'd just have to reimburse the company.

After swiping the card, he scrawled an electronic signature on the digital pad. The teenaged clerk thanked him in a desultory fashion and handed over the receipt, which Tyler stowed within his wallet, intending to send it to his personal accountant later, the same one who paid all his bills.

Tyler followed Charlotte as she pushed the cart toward the exit. Obviously intending to leave the cart with the elderly attendant, she began gathering up the plastic bags containing his purchases. He had forgotten that even in Aldrich stores most customers carried out their own bags.

"Here," he said, shouldering his way to the side of the cart. "Let me have the bags. You get the box."

"They're not heavy," she argued as he gathered the bags.

"They're heavier than the DVD player," he replied, the weight of them dangling at the ends of his arms. She bent and picked up the box from the bottom of the cart.

They walked through a double set of automatic doors and out onto the parking lot. Halfway to the car she suddenly asked, "Have you thought about how you're going to get all this home?"

He stopped dead in his tracks and looked over his shoulder with a sigh. "Guess I'd better go back in there and find a suitcase of some sort. Let's get this stuff to the car first."

They hurried to the far corner of the lot. He opened the trunk and got the goods stowed, then thoughtfully palmed the keys. "Can you drive a stick shift?"

She looked warily to the car. "Yes, but—"

"Okay, here's what we'll do," he interrupted, striding around to open the passenger door for her. "I'm going to drive up to the fire lane, then let you slide over to the wheel while I run back inside the store."

She lowered herself into the leather bucket, her expression troubled. Before she could voice her concerns, he closed the door and jogged around to the driver's side. She spoke as he dropped down behind the steering wheel.

"What if I have to move the car?"

"Then move it. Just come around again and pick me up." He started the engine and backed the car out of the space. "Don't worry," he told her. "It's a very forgiving transmission, built to take abuse. The worst that can happen is that you'll stall out." He saw the flash in her eye and chuckled. "I never thought you would stall. Just said it was the worst that could happen."

She smiled and pulled her braid over one shoulder. He wondered what her hair looked like down and if he would find out before he left here.

That thought nagged him as he left the idling car at the curb and literally raced back inside the store. He could almost see her with her bright, silky hair spread across her shoulders. She couldn't wear it in a braid all the time. Maybe he'd stick around until she let her hair down. At some point he'd accepted, without even considering, that he would stay on beyond the weekend, and he found a certain exhilarating freedom in that, but he couldn't really say why he'd decided to delay his departure.

Curiosity had a lot to do with it. This small-town

life seemed both more complicated and at the same time infinitely more simple than his own existence. He'd thought a lot, strictly from a business perspective, about how the other half lived, so to speak, but he saw now that he hadn't gotten a very clear picture from all those studies and reports he'd read.

As he'd strolled these aisles earlier he'd told himself that it was high time he actually experienced what the average shopper did, if only to better inform his business decisions. These shoppers, after all, made up his company's market, too, but they had lives outside these stores, and understanding more about that would undoubtedly prove a huge asset. In that way, this unintended sojourn was turning out to be an invaluable learning tool. But something else kept him here, too, something personal.

He couldn't quite put his finger on it, but for some reason that he didn't really understand, he needed this time away from his own life. He needed to *not* be himself for a little while. Maybe he needed to do nothing for a time, to literally loaf around and just watch the world go by.

He actually liked spending time with the Jefford family. Even Holt, as distrustful as he might be. Tyler had the feeling that they could give him a real, honest look at what a normal, healthy family should be. For a fellow who had never even known his own grandparents except in the most peripheral fashion, that suddenly seemed important.

Perhaps that explained why the warm, patient goodness of Hap Jefford so compelled Tyler, but then so did the fierce but companionable protectiveness of a self-assured, much-adored big brother like Holt. It amazed Tyler that he should have so little in common with these folks and still find such welcome and acceptance in their company—and without the least bit of fawning. That went for everyone, including the good citizens of Eden and its environs, despite his fears on that score.

Was it any wonder that he wanted to stay just a little longer?

He located the correct aisle and spent all of three minutes choosing a cheap but adequate nylon suitcase on rollers, which he paid for with the credit card.

After waiting several long minutes to get through the express checkout line, he jogged back out to the car, still idling next to the curb, and tossed the suitcase into the back while a trio of young men in ball caps, oversized jeans and tattered athletic shoes blatantly ogled the vehicle.

"Nice ride," one of them called.

Tyler smiled as he closed the trunk. "Thanks."

"Yours?"

"Yep."

"Who's that chick driving?" another of them asked.

"I wouldn't let *my* girl drive a car like that," the third declared at the same time.

My girl, Tyler thought, surprised when a hole seemed to open up inside his chest. He couldn't remember a time when he'd thought of a woman, or had wanted to think of a woman, as *his girl.* Neither could he recall a time when the woman in question hadn't been angling for just that. Until now.

On pure impulse, he headed to the passenger door, quipping, "You're hanging out with the wrong kind of woman, then, son."

The guys laughed, elbowing each other, and Tyler dropped down into the passenger seat. Closing the door, he looked to Charlotte and reached back for the safety belt.

"Let's go."

She tilted her head, studying him for a moment as if he were some strange kind of new bug. He buckled the belt.

"Come on. Move it. I have an early appointment in the morning." He smiled to let her know that he really wanted her to drive.

After a long moment, she faced forward again. "Okay." She put the transmission in gear and pulled away from the curb.

Tyler sat back and enjoyed the ride, noting with pleasure from the corner of his eye her little nods and shrugs of approval as she worked through the gears. By the time they'd made their way through numerous traffic lights along the bypass to the open road, Tyler's grin stretched clear across his face.

"What do you think?"

"Drives like a hundred-thousand bucks," she said.

"One-forty, actually," he corrected.

She boggled her eyes at him. "You can buy a house for that, a nice house, not to mention all of the good you could do with that kind of money. Think of all the poor people in the world!"

Disappointed, even a little wounded, he looked out the window. "So you think it's wrong of me to spend that kind of money on a car, then?"

"I didn't say that. It's just—"

"What about the guy who sold me this car? The people who built it? The parts suppliers and their families? What about the immigrant worker who cleans the dealership's building at night? By buying this car I keep them all in business."

"You're right, you're right," she conceded. "It's not my place to judge you, anyway, and I'm not, truly."

"If you say so, but I'll have you know that I give away something like a third of my income every year."

She glanced over at him then, shamefaced. "I'm sorry. It's just…your kind of money is a foreign concept to people like me."

"That goes both ways, you know," he said softly. "When I look at you—" He broke off, uncertain how to phrase it.

"What?"

He wouldn't tell her that he envied her. She

wouldn't believe him. He wouldn't tell her that he thought her beautiful, either. She would believe that even less, although it was the truth. Her beauty shone from the inside out with a purity that he admired in a way he couldn't even describe. He didn't want her to think that he was coming on to her, though, not after what that kid had said back there in the parking lot.

"You and your family," he said, choosing his words with honesty and care, "you're happy together. You love one another. That's something I've seen only rarely. I hope you know what it's worth."

"I do," she said, her hands tightening on the steering wheel. "Believe me, I do."

She drove on in silence. He rode beside her in quiet awareness, gradually relaxing as the miles fell away until delight somehow captured him again. He couldn't say why he found this so pleasant, but part of it, he knew, had to do with the assumption and words of that young man back there in the parking lot.

Charlotte was not his girl and she never would be. Looking at her softly lit profile against the night-blackened window, though, he had to admit that he'd been less than honest with himself about his decision to stay in Eden. He stayed because he couldn't help himself.

She drew him like a lodestone. Her honesty, her generosity, her simplicity, her contentment, they all called to him, along with some other indefinable quality that he couldn't begin to name. Despite her rough clothing and almost corny hairstyle, her lack of cosmetics or adornment of any sort, she somehow seemed to grow more beautiful every time he looked at her. He wanted to know her, to really know her.

Of course, nothing could or would come of it. Any fool knew that much. She was not the sort of woman he might escort to a business dinner or gala social occasion, and he didn't have time or the inclination for routinely hanging out a hundred and fifty miles from home. But for now, just for now, he'd allow himself to admire and to enjoy and maybe even to imagine what it might be like if she were his girl.

Unfortunately, he could never allow it to go further than that. He didn't want to hurt her, and he knew instinctively that Charlotte was the sort of woman who would expect more than he could give her. And rightly so. He wouldn't change that or anything else about her, but in all honesty she just didn't fit into his world, which meant that she wouldn't fit into his life, either, not after he left here.

Nevertheless, they seemed to be forging a friendship, something personal and private that belonged wholly to just the two of them and this moment. He'd never had that before, not with anyone, and he wanted this time in Eden with her and her family— and away from his own.

In an odd fashion that he didn't really understand, something told him that he could go home again in a few days more whole than he'd been when he'd arrived. Surely, he could have that much before he returned to his life.

Couldn't he?

Charlotte took a guilty pleasure in being behind the wheel of Tyler's massively expensive sports car. Compared to this, Hap's old diesel truck drove like a horse and buggy. That was not what discomfited her, though.

She'd never been so aware of anyone as she was of Tyler. She felt his gaze, felt his silent regard, and after she'd insulted him, too. Money had never meant beans to her, one way or another, and now suddenly she found herself judging him at every turn just because he'd been born into a wealthy family. It made her feel small and frightened in a manner that she didn't want to examine too closely.

"Can I ask you something?" she said into the velvety silence.

"Sure."

"What's it like to grow up with all that money?"

She felt rather than heard his sigh. He turned his gaze out the window. After a moment he said, "It just is, like the color of your hair or the face you see in the mirror every morning. It's not something you think about until someone else makes an issue of it."

She bit her lip at that. "I see. I'm sorry."

He shook his head. "Honest curiosity is one thing. Envy is something else altogether." She felt his gaze on her again. "And you really don't envy me, do you?"

Unsure how best to answer that, she wrinkled her nose apologetically. "Not really."

"Mind if I ask why?"

She had to think about that. "Well, it's not as if a few extra bucks wouldn't come in handy now and then," she said carefully, "but we already have all we need and...I don't know. I guess after your folks die you learn that what's most important is family, the people you love."

Tyler studied her for a moment. "My father used to say that everyone had their own treasure. Identify that, he would say, and you'd know how to work them."

"Work them?"

"You know, get the upper hand."

"Ah. Like in a business deal."

"Yeah, like in a business deal. Except I think he'd find you a tough nut to crack."

She let her eyes leave the roadway then and settle briefly on his face. "Why's that?"

"Because what you treasure most is unassailable," he said softly. "If my family cared for me one fraction of what yours does for you..."

You'd be a happy man, she thought. Stricken, she concentrated on the roadway again, wishing that she didn't know half so much as she did.

Chapter Eight

"Nah, come on. We'll all go together," Holt insisted, holding open the back door to the double-cab truck. "The parking's limited over at the church."

Shrugging, Tyler pocketed his car keys and started across the pavement.

"Wouldn't want to ding up that expensive mechanical wonder of yours," Holt added as soon as Tyler stepped off.

Tyler kept his tongue fixed firmly behind his teeth, partly because Holt was right and it embarrassed him, partly because the car would have drawn more unwanted attention his way. He already felt terribly out of place.

His new clothing felt odd, too light and too big and too...textured, somehow. Compared to Holt, however, who stood there in dark, creased jeans, a plain white shirt open at the collar and a brown leather coat with a western cut, Tyler appeared over-dressed. The leather jacket didn't quite match Holt's hat or boots, but Tyler had to admit that it fit the tall cowboy far better than his own tweedy sport coat fit him.

Before Tyler reached the truck, Charlotte came through the kitchen door. To Tyler's great delight, she'd left her hair loose. It hung halfway down her back in a sleek, satiny fall that put him in mind of a sunset in those glorious moments suspended between day and evening. The narrow black headband that held her vibrant hair back from her forehead emphasized the gentle widow's peak that gave her smiling face the shape of a slender heart.

Stopping in his tracks, he admired not only her hair and face but the slender length of her legs beneath her simple, straight gray skirt. He recognized her shoes with their rounded toes and delicate, modest heels, having noticed them on the shelves at the discount store. A pale peach twin set completed her ensemble. The whole of it probably cost her less than forty dollars, judging by what he'd seen last night, and he remarked fiercely to himself that she deserved better than that.

In fact, he could give her better, the very best, and would enjoy doing so, if only she would let him, which he knew without a doubt she would not.

For one thing, Charlotte wouldn't want expensive clothing. He knew only too well how she viewed his costly goods. His things didn't impress her at all, not his clothing, not his car. Instead, she made him feel a little ashamed about how he spent his money, even though he could easily afford to spend whatever he liked and gave generously to numerous charities.

It hardly mattered that he could buy Charlotte the best of everything, anyway. Designer labels could do nothing to enhance her loveliness. Charlotte's beauty came from inside and radiated outward with a purity that no amount of money could purchase.

For a long moment, Tyler stood as if mesmerized. Then the screen door banged, drawing him back to himself. Ducking his head self-consciously, he started forward again. A moment later, he realized that Hap had joined them.

Clad in shiny, threadbare brown dress slacks, a navy-blue shirt, loosely knotted gray tie, red suspenders and a dark red cardigan sweater, he parked a jaunty gray fedora on his head, cupping the brim downward in front with a slick, sweeping motion of one hand. Tyler laughed, finding an odd joy in just looking at the old fellow. He mentally shook his head as he spied the thin white socks worn with stiff black wingtips as Holt helped Hap up into the truck.

Tyler moved to Charlotte's side, asking conversationally, "Who's minding the store?"

"No one. We don't staff the front desk on Sundays, but we don't turn away guests when we're here, either."

Tyler opened the front passenger door for her,

noting that even as she thanked him she slid a loaded look her brother's way. Holt's mouth fixed in a straight line. After donning a pair of sunshades, he slipped behind the wheel. Tyler climbed into the backseat with Hap, wondering if he had become a bone of contention between brother and sister. The idea pinched a little.

Overcome with the scent of cheap aftershave as soon as he shut the door, he glanced at Hap, realizing that he had never before seen the old man cleanly shaved. His expression must have shown his shock, for Hap grinned ear-to-ear.

"Clean up good, don't I?"

"You sure do," Tyler replied, marveling at the happiness that radiated off the old man. Thankfully, Holt cracked open the window up front and quickly got them moving, bringing enough breeze into the vehicle to freshen the air.

Breathing easier, Tyler took time to study the elder Jefford. Crippled with arthritis and plagued with other ailments, he had lost his wife and only child while living a life of hard work that had apparently left him without two nickels to rub together. Given all that, Hap should have been the last man to live in such joy that it overflowed, making it a pleasure just to sit next to him. Tyler had to wonder how that could be.

Mere minutes later, Holt pulled the long truck into the grass beside the park on Mesquite Street across from the small, white clapboard church that

Tyler had noticed the day before. The sign above the door declared it to be simply, First Church of Eden.

They all piled out and came together at the edge of the street. A relatively well-dressed, dark-haired man standing beneath an ancient hickory tree in front of the church waved in greeting and came to meet them as they crossed to the sidewalk. He clapped Holt on the shoulder, engulfed Charlotte in a hug, then did the same with Hap, kissing the old man on the cheek.

"How're you doing, Granddad? You look good."

Without waiting for an answer, he turned his attention to Tyler. Seeing only interest and welcome in the other man's familiar hazel eyes, Tyler put out his hand while Charlotte made the introductions.

"Ryan, this is Tyler Aldrich. He's staying with us. Tyler, this is our brother, Ryan."

Though he stood a couple inches shorter than Holt, Ryan had maybe thirty pounds on his brother, making him seem the larger of the two men. Fit and strong, with dark, chestnut-brown hair and dressed in a smart navy suit, dress shoes, striped shirt and tie, he might have been any executive anywhere.

"Good to meet you, Ty," he exclaimed, shaking Tyler's hand with both of his. People rarely addressed Tyler as Ty, not even as a boy. His mother would have objected vociferously, but Tyler said nothing. It fit somehow in this setting.

Obviously used to being in charge, Ryan moved behind the group and gently but firmly herded them toward the church, saying, "We're going to need some extra space. Sis, you go in first. Granddad, I know you want to sit on the aisle because scooting across the pew hurts you, so you come in at the back here."

"Yes, sir, Mr. Jefford," Holt teased. "Anything you say, Mr. Jefford."

"Now, don't give me any of your lip," Ryan scolded lightly, sounding more and more like the assistant principal he was. "I'm just trying to help."

While the brothers bickered good-naturedly, Tyler took the opportunity to slide into place behind Charlotte, feeling Holt fall in behind him, just like students in school. They stepped up onto the single, broad stoop and pushed into the crowded building as a group.

Surprised to find that the sanctuary contained no foyer, Tyler spent the next fifteen minutes shaking hands and nodding at folks whose names he barely caught as the group worked their way toward the front pews. He followed Charlotte into the narrow space between the second and third pews and took a seat next to her on the unpadded bench. Holt folded himself up next to Tyler and parked the hat, which he had removed as soon as they'd entered the building, on one bent knee.

Tyler took a moment to look around him. Talk about bare bones. Walls, floor, pews, all were constructed of pale wood finished with an oil rub that had to be decades old. Only the platform at the front boasted carpet in a bright peacock-blue, which contrasted sharply with the white painted lectern, altar and three armless chairs.

An acoustic guitar had been propped against an old upright piano in one corner, and hanging fixtures of cheap, unpolished brass lit the room. The tall, narrow windows had been painted in swirls of blue, green and gold, softening the austere interior. A fresh flower arrangement of red carnations supplied the only other splash of color.

A young woman in an ankle-length black knit dress, her pale hair twisted up against the back of her head, moved forward and took a seat at the piano. She opened her sheet music and began to play softly, prompting those visiting in the aisles and over the backs of the pews to take their seats and ebb into silence.

Grover Waller, dressed in a severe black suit that did nothing to alter his jovial appearance, hurried forward and occupied one of the chairs on the platform. A tall, gaunt younger fellow and a stout middle-aged woman joined him. After a few moments, the music stopped, and the young man stepped up to welcome everyone and make announcements.

The gutters on the "education building" needed cleaning. Next Sunday everyone should bring a dish to the monthly potluck dinner. For November no potluck dinner had been scheduled due to the annual Thanksgiving feast. Sign-up sheets could be found on the narrow tables at the back of the sanctuary. The youth would be taking the church van to a movie in Duncan on the following Saturday evening. Everyone was encouraged to attend the football game on Friday and cheer on the local team at home.

Next came announcements from the congregation. First one and then another stood to proclaim good news. This one's daughter had won the lead in the school play. That one's son had been elected to student council. A plump woman with suspiciously dark hair stood to declare that she had *finally* become a grandmother. The nineteen-inch-long, seven-pound infant resided in Houston with her parents. An older couple stood to be applauded for celebrating fifty-four years of marriage. Several confessed to birthdays during the coming week, at which point the crowd spontaneously broke into congratulatory song, accompanied by the piano.

Finally Grover stepped into the pulpit to call the congregation to worship with prayer. Tyler dutifully bowed his head, but he soon found himself looking up in surprise as Grover took on the authoritative tone of a true man of God. Tyler noticed that several people had lifted their hands toward heaven. He'd never seen that before.

Tyler had attended church often enough, mainly whenever it had seemed necessary or expedient. His family held membership at one of the oldest, most notable churches in Dallas, and there had been many weddings, funerals and baptisms over the years. He'd always found it a pleasant, restful experience filled with beautiful music and formal speech. On occasion he'd even felt an odd tug at his heart, but he'd never felt this sense of community.

More revelations followed. The gaunt fellow went to strap on the guitar, while the stout woman moved to the front of the platform to lead the music. And such music! It was so exuberant that Tyler actually felt a bit uncomfortable at times, though he had to admit that those around him seemed to be having fun.

Four men took up an offering before Grover returned to the pulpit to preach because, he later joked, stepping on toes tended to close wallets. Tyler dropped a hundred dollars into the plate when it came by, wishing he could have doubled the amount, but with a mere seventeen bucks in cash left in his pocket, he'd have to visit an ATM soon. If he could find one.

Grover Waller proved to be a huge surprise. Tyler had liked the round, friendly, soft-spoken man when he'd gotten to know him the day before at the dominoes table, but Waller hadn't quite fit Tyler's idea of a clergyman. That idea changed fast. Grover didn't preach so much as he taught, didn't exhort so much as encourage, yet he was blunt to the point of shocking, at least to Tyler's way of thinking.

"Your sin is no different from the sin of the worst mass murderer in history," he declared. "In God's eyes, sin is sin, brothers and sisters. It is the great equalizer. Don't go congratulating yourselves because you don't do what some others do or because some folks think you're pretty swell. If you have not found the saving grace of Jesus Christ, you're no different in God's eyes than anyone else. And if you have received that grace, you really have no excuse for not living a life pleasing to your Heavenly Father."

The preacher went on to speak about the Holy Spirit and matters that Tyler frankly did not understand, but those first words tied up his mind to the point that he couldn't really even think about anything else. He realized with some shock that in a far corner of his mind he'd always thought that he was somehow different from everyone else. He was Tyler Aldrich.

Too often in his business dealings he'd encountered exaggerations and outright lies, so he prided himself on his honesty. God knew that he didn't steal, as so many did, padding accounts and invoices. But then why would he since he'd always had anything and everything money could buy in the first place?

Okay, he didn't outright lie, but he did expect others to take his word at face value and agree with it, which they usually did—everyone but his family, who had no respect for his position. But why shouldn't his word be accepted? He was Tyler Aldrich of *the* Aldriches, CEO of Aldrich & Asso-

ciates Grocery. And here stood this man telling him
that his smallest evasion was judged just as harshly
by God as the worst case of mass murder.

The idea took Tyler's breath away, and suddenly
the snobbery for which he had so long condemned
his mother and sister seemed as much a problem for
him as for them. Why should the Aldriches be better
than anyone else? Could his honesty be of any more
value than another man's? More valuable than
Holt's or Hap's or Charlotte's? If his sin was no different than anyone else's, how could his goodness
be?

And what about this grace of which Grover
spoke?

Tyler paid little attention to the remainder of the
service, so caught up with this idea of his sin being
as bad everyone else's in the whole wide world that
he couldn't concentrate on more immediate events.
He considered the possibility that Grover had con-
cocted this sermon just for him, but try as he might,
the startling concept of equality in God's eyes
wouldn't let him go.

*You're no different in God's eyes than anyone
else.*

By the time he managed to shift mental gears, he
and the Jeffords were standing outside beneath a
darkening sky. A few people headed straight for
their automobiles, but most clustered in small
groups, talking and laughing.

Almost immediately a bunch of young people

surrounded Ryan, who seemed quite popular with his students. They all evidently knew Hap, too, who teased and joked with them.

Several men approached Holt, stepping aside for a moment of conversation. That left Tyler with Charlotte, which suited him just fine.

A number of people engaged them in passing, several pausing to shake Tyler's hand again and thank him for visiting, and then a tall, solidly built fellow with a toddler, a girl, parked in the crook of one elbow stepped up to Charlotte. Garbed in a white shirt and tie, sans jacket, with blond hair falling rakishly over one brow, he literally radiated fondness—and something more.

"Why, Jerry!" Charlotte exclaimed, stretching upward to press her cheek to his. "I didn't expect to see you until the holidays."

"Sandy's mom is having new flooring installed at her house. We came down to help her move stuff out of the way."

Charlotte spent several moments fussing over the child, who cuddled shyly against her father's shoulder with her thumb in her mouth. "She's just so adorable."

"You're looking good."

Smiling, Charlotte rocked up onto her toes. "Thanks. So are you."

Tyler was beginning to feel left out and more than a little miffed about it. Who, he wondered, was Jerry, and what did he mean to Charlotte? Tyler sensed a history here, and he didn't like it, especially considering that light in Jerry's eyes.

"Is Sandy with you?" Charlotte asked.

"No, she's sleeping in this morning. Every little thing seems to sap her strength these days."

"Oh? I hope she's not ill."

Jerry smiled. "Actually she's pregnant again."

"How wonderful!"

"We're hoping for a boy this time."

"Wouldn't that be perfect!"

Suddenly everything changed. It was as if lightning had struck but no one felt it except the three of them, Charlotte and Jerry, who stood looking into each other's eyes, and Tyler, who stood staring at them.

"You should be a mother," Jerry said softly, and in that instant Tyler *knew,* even before Jerry guiltily switched his gaze to Tyler himself.

Ignoring Jerry's last statement, Charlotte slipped an arm through Tyler's. "What a ninny. I was just so surprised to see you I didn't think to introduce Tyler."

She hastened to give the men each other's names without a single word of explanation. Jerry nodded in acknowledgment just as a light rain began to fall.

"I'd better get her back to her grandmother's," he said, laying a protective hand over the child's head.

"Give my best to Sandy," Charlotte called as he moved away.

Before the fellow was out of earshot, Holt joined

them, people scattering in every direction. Hap headed for the truck as Ryan took off at a jog for the parking area in the rear of the building. Tyler could do nothing except hurry Charlotte toward the pickup. Holt caught up to Hap and held his arm as they crossed the street. Tyler yanked open the rear door and handed Charlotte inside, leaving the front seat for Hap this time.

"Whew! Weather's turned off nasty," Hap observed in his gravelly voice as Tyler slid in next to Charlotte.

"I'm surprised it held off this long," Holt commented.

Tyler realized that he wasn't going to get an opportunity to find out about Jerry Moody and just what the man meant to Charlotte. He felt a petty, sick resentment over that. Looking down at his damp jacket, he could only shake his head.

What was wrong with him? So Charlotte had once had a boyfriend who'd married someone else. What difference did it make? Except it did, somehow. In a very stupid, selfish, inane way, it even hurt.

They pulled up at the motel, and Holt killed the engine, declaring, "I can smell that ham from here, sis."

Tyler immediately became aware of his empty stomach. He'd skipped breakfast in order to be ready for church on time, and now he regretted that. He regretted, too, the thought of a lonely meal, and he absolutely hated the feeling of wanting to tag along with the Jeffords like some waif from another century.

Charlotte chuckled and said to no one in particular, "I guess you're smelling those potatoes and gravy, too."

"Nothing better than red-eye gravy," Hap declared, opening up his door.

Holt hurried around to assist his grandfather, but Charlotte stayed where she was for a moment, gazing over at Tyler with calm eyes. "You've got time to change, if you want, but don't take too long at it."

Tyler felt his heart thud. "I'm invited to dinner?"

"Well, of course you are," she said, hopping out of the truck, "and I expect you to eat it while it's hot." She dashed for the kitchen door, leaving him alone in the truck.

So he was *expected* for dinner, was he?

He smiled.

Funny, he'd never realized that the sun could shine even in the gloom of rain.

Chapter Nine

Ryan sat back with a satisfied sigh and patted his firm middle. "Sis, it is downright sinful the way you cook."

"I'd have to say it's delectable," Tyler remarked, smiling up at her.

He'd been doing that a lot, smiling at her, and every time her heart rate kicked up another notch. She didn't know when she'd decided to include Tyler in Sunday dinner. It just didn't occur to her not to. Even before Jerry had surprised her on the church lawn, she'd taken it for granted that Tyler would be at her dinner table. If it had seemed more important that he be there after she'd talked to Jerry, well, she wouldn't think about that now. Obviously the rest of the family had expected Tyler to join them because not even Holt had said a contrary word when Ty had walked in. Ryan especially seemed to enjoy his company.

Always less intense and more trustful than Holt, Ryan's easy, open-armed acceptance of this newcomer in their midst came as no surprise. He took after Hap in that way. Still, Charlotte wondered if perhaps Hap had said something to Ryan about Tyler, something to make Ryan think that she had feelings for Tyler or vice versa, but somehow she didn't think he had.

She thanked the men for their compliments and rose to begin clearing the table. Ty immediately jumped to his feet, but Charlotte quickly refused his help.

"No, no. I'm going to clear and stack, but the boys always wash up on Sundays. Don't you, guys?"

Holt shot to his feet and headed toward the lobby, saying, "Right after the game."

"What he means," Ryan clarified, rising more decorously, "is right after we eat the leftovers for supper." He clapped a hand onto Tyler's shoulder, saying, "You do like football, don't you?"

Tyler nodded, seemingly torn between helping her and watching the football game. Hap got up and hobbled after Holt, saying, "Come on, there, boys. We got a tradition to uphold here."

Charlotte made a shooing motion with one hand, and Tyler finally relented. She tried not to be flattered that he appeared to prefer clearing the table with her to watching the game with her brothers.

Ryan, being the more enthusiastic of the two,

pushed ahead, leaving Ty to bring up the rear. Charlotte couldn't help glancing in his direction—or admiring the way those new jeans fit him.

She bowed her head, confused by her own reactions and thoughts. Could it be that God was trying to tell her something? Shaking her head, she rejected all possibility that God might intend Tyler Aldrich to become more than a pleasant interlude in her life.

She and Ty lived in two completely different worlds. His kind of life terrified her. How awful it would be to constantly fear not fitting in. Conversely, the idea that a rich man from the big city would find her lifestyle appealing was nothing less than laughable. Besides, he'd given her no real signal that he found her more than a curiosity.

Feeling incredibly foolish, she quickly cleared the table, stowed the leftovers to be reheated later and stacked the dishes to be washed. Then she removed her apron, dislodging the headband in the process. She smoothed her hair back from her forehead, replaced the headband, tugged at her jeans and turned toward the door. Sucking in a deep breath, she pasted on a smile and went to join the men.

Holt had stretched out on one of the sofas, his booted feet propped on the arm, while Hap occupied the rocking chair as usual, and Ryan sat at one end of the remaining couch, his gaze fixed on the television screen. Tyler had taken the other end, leaving only the middle of the sofa for her, unless she chose to pull out one of the straight chairs around the game table. That seemed rude somehow, telling, so she went to sit next to Ty. No sooner did she lower herself to the cushion than Ryan jumped up, hollering with glee. At the same time Tyler leaned forward, laughing, and Holt bolted into an upright position.

"I guess our team scored," she commented brightly.

Tyler sat back, casually lifting an arm about her shoulders as he turned to address her. "That's twice in eight minutes!" He looked to Holt, exclaiming, "Now tell me the quarterback is too young."

"That doesn't mean the coach isn't too old," Charlotte pointed out.

Tyler looked at her in surprise. A smile spread slowly across his face. "You think the coach is too old, do you? I'll be sure to tell him you said so."

"You know the coach?" she asked, wondering why she should be surprised.

"Ty has a box," Ryan announced pointedly.

"You mean a private box at the stadium?" Charlotte clarified.

"It's the company's box," Tyler said lightly.

"We're all going to go down to join him for a game sometime," Holt commented in a dry tone.

Charlotte doubted that very much. For one thing, all of them never went anywhere together except church; someone had to take care of things around here. Besides, she couldn't believe that either Hap or Holt would ever willingly make the drive to Dallas. Ryan would jump all over any actual invitation, and she hoped he got one, but chances were that Tyler Aldrich would forget all about them as soon as he left here. And that was for the best.

Talk continued in a lively vein, the men arguing the merits of various elements of the team. Charlotte had her own opinions, and she quietly interjected them into the conversation. Several minutes passed before they all settled down again. Only then did Charlotte realize that Ty had never removed his arm from about her shoulders and that she'd somehow shifted closer to him.

She contemplated moving away, but she didn't want to call attention to the situation, especially as no one else even seemed to notice. After some time, she allowed herself to relax and get caught up in the enjoyment of the game and just sharing space with those dear to her. Only later did she question the wisdom of including Tyler Aldrich in that category.

Tyler sat forward on the couch and clasped his hands together between his knees, forearms resting on his thighs. The Jefford men had trooped en masse to the kitchen, looking for food now that the football game had ended. How they could even think of eating, he didn't understand, but he appreciated the opportunity to be alone with Charlotte, all the same.

Now that it was just the two of them, though, he

didn't quite know what to say. The Jeffords as a whole were easy people to be around. Hap treated him almost like family, while Ryan already seemed to think of him as a good buddy. Even Holt, who at times acted like he expected Ty to make off with the family silver, obviously bore him no ill will. Their welcoming acceptance frankly floored him. No doubt they treated everyone else the same way, but Tyler still reveled in their friendship.

Only Charlotte confused him. She couldn't have been more welcoming, caring or generous, but that just seemed part of her nature. It shamed him to think that his own family would not be so accepting of a stranger. Rather than friendliness and inclusion, snobbery, conflict and rivalry characterized the Aldriches. They would look down on the Jeffords without a doubt, Charlotte included. Charlotte especially. So what was he doing here with her? What was the point? And why did her reasons for being here with him matter so much?

Tyler really wanted to believe that all the Jeffords simply liked him, that they found him special somehow, apart from his sky box and millions of dollars. But he couldn't help wondering if his wealth figured into it, although in Charlotte's case he suspected she liked him *despite* his money. Maybe that was the key. Maybe the others were willing to give him the benefit of the doubt simply because Charlotte liked him. Tyler couldn't fault them for that.

"That was a great game," she finally said.

"Oh, yeah. It's always a great game when they win."

The woman amazed him. Not only did she look like a vision, work like a Trojan, cook like a chef, treat all who came into her orbit with compassion and welcome and quietly, effortlessly order her entire family, the girl also knew a thing or two about football.

She had a coach for a brother, so Tyler supposed he shouldn't have been surprised. What really blew him away, though, was how much she seemed to actually enjoy the game for its own sake.

On the other hand, she seemed to enjoy everything in the same way—her family, her work, her faith, her whole life. That she could do so when she'd suffered so much loss and had so little made Tyler feel small and spoiled.

He admired her, but it was more than that, too. He wanted for himself what she had, her contentment, her goodness. Worse, he wanted her in his life somehow.

It was a foolish notion, but sitting next to her here on the sofa with his arm curled about her slender shoulders earlier had felt like the most natural thing in the world to him. It shouldn't have—no one could have been more out of place kicking back to watch a televised football game than the one person in the room who usually watched those home games live from a private box for twelve on the fifty-yard line.

No doubt Charlotte would feel as out of place there as he often did here, but somehow that didn't seem to matter anymore.

Glancing through the picture window to the front lawn and the roadway beyond, he saw that the rain had stopped and the sky had cleared. In perhaps an hour, night would descend. Time enough for a little exploration.

"I don't know about you, but I could use some exercise," he said, swinging his head around to look at her. She sat tucked back into the corner of the leather sofa recently vacated by Ryan, one leg curled beneath the other. Her elbow braced against the rolled arm as she toyed idly with a sleek strand of her hair. "Want to take a little walk?"

She hesitated. He could see her mind working, though what thoughts went through that fine brain of hers he couldn't have said. After a moment, she nodded. He hadn't realized that his heart had stopped beating until it started again. Straightening, he rose at once to his feet, giving her no time to rethink. Charlotte unfolded her legs and got up, moving silently to the apartment door.

He followed and listened as she explained to her family that they were going to the park. Reaching inside, she took a corduroy coat from the chair in the corner behind the door and handed it to him, then removed a smaller down-filled nylon jacket from a peg on the wall. She threw on the dark blue nylon jacket as they walked toward the front porch.

Tyler held the outer door wide as she passed through and turned toward the ramp.

"You'll want to wear that," she said, glancing back over her shoulder at the corduroy coat that he carried in one hand.

He didn't argue, just shrugged into the heavy corduroy. The temperature outside had dropped considerably. The coat smelled of Hap so must have been the old man's. Ty found it a cheery, comfortable aroma. Falling into step beside her, he strolled across the pavement. He felt good, as if enfolded in a warm hug, but something else percolated just below the surface of his mind, too.

Hope, he decided after a moment. He felt hopeful, eager, even excited. All the frustration that had driven him from Dallas only days earlier seemed distant and foreign, as if it belonged to another lifetime, another man. Smiling, he sucked in a great lungful of autumn air, content to amble along as she led him around the back of the motel and across a patch of open ground to the point where Mesquite Street came to a dead end.

The entrance to the park lay some three blocks distant, so they strolled in that direction. Despite the increasingly stark trees, the park couldn't have seemed more beautiful to him if it had been the true Garden of Eden, and he wouldn't have complained if the walk had been three miles instead of three blocks.

In ways he could not have planned or even understood before, this sojourn in Eden, Oklahoma, seemed to be exactly what he needed. The peace and tranquility alone had reenergized him, and he'd gotten a good, hard look at how the majority of the world lived. In addition to that, the Jeffords had shown him what family could be. But might there be something more to it, something deep and personal? Somehow, he had begun to hope so.

Charlotte folded her arms, holding her jacket closed against the chill. Striking out on foot like this might well be foolhardy. The rain had cleared for the moment, but those clouds in the northwest promised more. Her chief concern, however, did not involve the weather.

She shouldn't be doing this. Being alone with Tyler courted disaster. She supposed that seeing Jerry with his little daughter today had made her feel that she'd missed out on something, but that was no reason to behave foolishly. She sensed Tyler's growing interest in her, though, and right now that made him very nearly irresistible. Disaster indeed.

Tyler Aldrich could have any woman he wanted. With his wealth, connections, charm and looks, he probably found himself inundated with interested women. She was nothing more than the woman of the moment, and she'd best remember that. No one could seriously expect that his interest in her could be more than curiosity or that they could have any sort of future together.

In all likelihood he'd probably never met a less sophisticated individual than her, and as alien as he at times seemed in her world, she knew that she would be even more lost in his. The man had a private luxury box at the pro football stadium in Dallas, for pity's sake. He knew the coach personally! She wouldn't know how to behave rubbing elbows with people like that.

No, she couldn't see anything ahead for her and Tyler Aldrich, and she wouldn't set herself up for disappointment by trying to create anything. She knew, had always known, that her life lay here in Eden with her grandfather and brothers. When Tyler left this place, as he must soon do, that would be the end of it. Period.

God had surely brought him here for a purpose, however. She'd sensed some confusion on his part during the pastor's sermon that morning, and this walk seemed like a good opportunity to clear up any questions he might have about what the pastor had said. Letting her feet take care of getting them to the park, she turned her mind to the better subject.

"I keep thinking about Grover's sermon today."

Tyler zipped her a look from the corners of his eyes. "Yeah. Yeah, that was interesting."

"Anything about it strike you especially?"

He put his head down for a moment. "I've sort of been thinking about the equality thing."

That set her back enough to slow her steps. "Equality?"

"Sure. You know, how everyone's sin is really the same."

Picking up the pace again, she mulled that over. She'd never thought of it in terms of equality, but that did make a certain sense. "Hap says that the only difference between people is Jesus," she remarked.

"I wouldn't say that's the only difference," Tyler replied with a smile. "Hap may be the most gentle and caring fellow I've ever met."

Pleased, she bumped his shoulder with hers. "I meant, the only difference in God's eyes."

Tyler's brow furrowed. "You don't think God sees what kind of person Hap is?"

"Of course. I also believe that God honors the good we do," she clarified. "The point is that, since all sin is equal in God's eyes, we're all equally guilty, so we all need the grace that comes to us through Jesus Christ."

"Okay. I get that," Tyler said slowly.

She could tell from his tone that he wondered where she might be going with this, and ultimately she supposed the only way to get there was just to ask what she wanted to know. "Are you a Christian, then, Ty?"

He shrugged. "Sure. My family have been members of one of the biggest, oldest churches in Dallas for generations."

"Then you understand what I mean by grace?" she asked. He made no reply, as if he took her question to be a statement. After a moment, she went on uneasily. "I guess what I want to know is why you haven't given your pain and grief to God."

He looked genuinely confused at that. "I beg your pardon?"

She stopped, realizing only in that moment that they'd reached the entrance to the park, and turned to face him. She realized, too, that she'd spoken without thinking again, but now she had no choice except to blunder on.

"You don't seem to have yielded to God your grief over your father's death and the pain of your family's rejection," she said calmly, "and I can't help wondering why."

"The pain of my family's rejection?" he echoed, sounding genuinely confused. "Where on earth did you get that?"

She spread her hands helplessly. "From what you said about your brother and sister resenting that your father chose you to head the company. That has to feel like rejection."

He shook his head. "Sweetheart, I wouldn't know how to behave if my family wasn't always at each other's throats."

Dismayed for him, she tried to reconcile that statement with what she knew about family. "I understand that you're all probably only now coming to grips with the loss of your father and—"

"Please. It's not like he was a big part of our lives or anything."

Now she felt confused. "But he was your father."

"Let me tell you a little story," Tyler said, leading her over to a bench, where they sat down side by side. "I was maybe ten when the maid had to see somebody about something." He shrugged. "I guess she didn't want to leave me home alone. Anyway, I wound up riding along with her in her car to this strange neighborhood, and I guess we were there for some time because I started playing baseball in the streets with a bunch of kids I'd never met before. I hit this ball straight through the front window of a house there." He made a motion with his arm, indicating the path of a line dive.

"Oh, no." Charlotte lifted her hand to hide a smile. "I broke a window once, with a pork chop."

He chuckled. "A pork chop?"

She nodded and wrinkled her nose. "It was greasy, and when I stabbed at it with a fork, it flew off my plate and through the window."

"And what did your father do?" Ty asked.

She spread her hands. "Why, he fixed it. That window was always getting broken. The kitchen was really small and we didn't have a dining room so the table had to sit right up against it."

Tyler slumped back against the bench, shaking his head. "So you broke a window and your father fixed it. No big deal. I broke a window and my father sent me to boarding school for the rest of the year."

She gasped, appalled. "He didn't! Over a window that you broke accidentally?"

Tyler made a face, shaking his head. "The window didn't have anything to do with it. What infuriated him was that he had to be called out of an important business meeting to deal with it."

"But—"

"The maid gave them the number," Tyler went on. "I begged them not to call. I even offered to buy those people a new house if they wouldn't phone my father's office."

Charlotte snickered. She couldn't help it. "You really offered to buy them a whole new house?"

His lips twitched. "Hey, I was ten. Cut me a break here."

They laughed over that, then fell silent.

"It wasn't so bad, really," Tyler said after a moment. "Those months at boarding school taught me a lot of discipline. I fared better than the maid, that's for sure. She was fired on the spot." He sent Charlotte a rueful glance. "No one called my father out of a business meeting and got away with it. Business always came first with him. Always." He picked at a piece of lint on the pocket of Hap's coat. "Toward the end of their marriage my mother used to have him dragged out on the least pretext. I assume that was why he divorced her. One thing was certain, he was never there for us, any of us."

Reaching out, Charlotte laid her hand over his. "I'm so sorry, Tyler, but I do understand. My mother was like that in a way. It wasn't that she had more important things to do but that she seemed to think everyone else was there for her and not the other way around."

He turned his hand and clasped hers palm to palm. "Maybe we're not so different after all," he whispered.

Suddenly, she very much feared that he might be right.

Chapter Ten

They sat together in silence for a while, soaking in the serene beauty of the park, hands clasped but not looking at each other.

Finally, Tyler's soft voice asked, "How did your parents die? You said something about an oil-field accident."

Charlotte cleared her throat and answered him. "In my father's case, that's right. He fell from a derrick."

"That must have been tough," Ty murmured, squeezing her hand with his.

"It was a terrible shock, but not as shocking as what my mother did," Charlotte admitted.

She rarely spoke of it. In all the years since, she hadn't found any reason to tell another person about it. Everyone in the family and around town had always known. It had become common knowledge almost from the moment it had happened.

Ty squeezed her hand again. "What did she do?"

Charlotte looked at their clasped hands. The sight of them made her feel even sadder for some reason. "As soon as she got the news about Dad, my mother swallowed a bottle of pills." She matched her gaze to his then. "With zero regard for the children she was leaving behind, she took her own life. She wrote a note, asking, 'Who will take care of me now?'"

Tyler closed his eyes. "Oh, man." He lifted his free arm and curled it around her, pulling her close to his side. "I have to wonder how the human race survives sometimes."

"I know how I survived," Charlotte said, laying her head on his shoulder and letting herself feel comforted. "My grandparents taught me to take these things to the Lord." She lifted her head again. "I want to encourage you to do the same. It's like Grover said today, His grace is more than sufficient."

Tyler chuckled lightly and brushed his knuckles across her cheek. "I'd rather that you prayed for me, frankly."

She blinked and sat up straight again, pulling her hand free. "Yes, certainly, but you can always go to God yourself, you know."

"Somehow I think your prayers might serve me better."

For a moment she stared up at him. "Why would you say that?"

He smiled down at her, his palm cupping the curve of her jaw. "I suspect you have a direct line."

Flabbergasted, she exclaimed, "But don't you see that your prayers are as powerful as mine?"

"No," he answered simply, leaning closer still. "Now let me ask you something."

"All right."

"Would you ever consider leaving Eden?"

The shift in subject threw her. She'd expected something along spiritual lines. "Leave Eden?"

His sky-blue eyes held her. "To live, I mean. Would you ever consider living anywhere besides Eden?"

She didn't have to look for the answer, but it might have been more accurate to say that she didn't want to look for it. "No!"

He drew back a little. "Why not? You never know what another place might have to offer." Obviously warming to his subject, he rushed on. "Take Dallas, for instance. You could eat out every night of the year and never visit the same restaurant twice. And shopping. Oh, my goodness. You can't imagine what the shopping is like. Even I know it's far superior to anything around here. Then there's entertainment." He waved a hand. "Anything you can think of. Lots you probably wouldn't think of, too, but never mind that."

He went on enumerating all the reasons for living in the Dallas/Fort Worth Metroplex area. "The best hospitals, museums, art galleries, pro sports, amateur sports…" He threw up his hands. "You have no idea!"

"I'm sure it's lovely," she said, mystified, "but it's not for me."

"How can you know that?" he demanded, his gaze intense.

"Well, for one thing," she pointed out, quite unnecessarily, she thought, "my family is here, and they need me, Granddad especially."

"Your brothers are adults," Tyler argued. "They want you to be happy. Your grandfather, too, no doubt."

"But I'm happy here."

"Are you?"

"Absolutely. If I wasn't, I'd be married to Jerry Moody right now." Her hand rose halfway to her mouth, but the words had already been said, although why she had said them she didn't know.

Tyler sat back with a *whump.* "I knew it." Abruptly he shifted toward her, eyes narrowing. "You're still in love with him, aren't you?"

"No!" She shook her head, feeling out of control and reckless. "Why would you think that? I just told you that I broke off our engagement."

She could see the wheels turning in his head, the cogs fitting into place behind his eyes. "You broke off your engagement because Jerry wanted to move away from here."

"Eden is my home," she said, trembling now. "I belong here."

"And you don't love Jerry?" Ty probed.

For some reason, she had to make him believe her. "No," she said firmly. "I'm fond of him, but if I loved him…if I'd loved him *enough,* I'd have married him."

Ty's nostrils flared, and she knew suddenly that he was going to kiss her. She knew as well that she must stop him. She meant to. She truly did, but at that moment she couldn't think how. Instead, everything in her focused on the descent of his head and then the pressure of his lips on hers.

Her head fell back against his shoulder, and her eyes slammed closed. Without her consent her arms rose to slide about his neck. The whole world screeched to a halt and gradually tilted. Only Tyler anchored her to its surface, his arms looped around her, holding her against him.

Once she felt the world right itself again she blinked up at him, realizing where they were and just what they'd been doing. She gasped to think that she'd sat here in this very public place in broad— okay, waning—daylight, kissing Tyler Aldrich. Kissing!

"O-h-h." She slapped a hand over her mouth.

Tyler tilted his head as if measuring the effect of that kiss. After a moment, he grinned, his white, even teeth dazzling in the deepening gloom. Her face flamed. At almost the same instant, he tenderly pushed her head back down against her shoulder, as if to spare her the embarrassment.

She sat there for several moments before she understood that he was waiting for her to speak, but what could she say? What *should* she say? Moments ticked away before a truly coherent thought formed inside her head. Only then did she drop her hand from her mouth.

"Tyler," she said, sitting up and taking a firm grip on herself, "that should not have happened."

He lifted both eyebrows. "Why not?"

"B-because…" She blanched at the breathless sound of her own voice. Making a concerted effort to appear calm and unruffled, she put her concern into carefully chosen words. "That should not have happened because I'm not the sort of woman who casually does that kind of thing."

He laughed. Laughed. Sliding back on the seat, he lifted his face and laughed out loud. She frowned, offended but somehow uncertain about it, until he chucked her beneath the chin with a curved finger.

"Sweetheart," he said indulgently, "you are not like any other woman I've ever known, but, believe me, I do understand that much about you." He placed a hand over his heart, adding, "I absolutely meant no disrespect. You have to know that."

She did. Now that her pulse rate had normalized and her brain seemed to be functioning again, she knew that while he had initiated the kiss, he had also ended it. After a relatively short period of time.

She blushed, aware that she had overreacted.

In all likelihood that kiss had told him everything

he'd needed to know about her, and that would be the end of the matter.

Nodding, she looked around, relieved to note that they were quite alone. Apparently everyone else had the good sense to stay in out of the chancy weather. She turned a glance over one shoulder to take note of the clouds. Building high in the northwest, the dark gray matter now seemed to loom over them in the silvering light.

"We'd better get inside before it rains again," she stated firmly, pushing up to her feet once more. As if to reinforce that decision, a chill, damp breeze swirled around them.

Tyler stood, and they headed back in the direction from which they had come, both seemingly caught in their own thoughts.

Whatever God's reason for allowing their two universes to meld for this moment in time, Charlotte told herself firmly, that's all it was, all it could ever be, a moment in time. Tyler would soon leave, and their paths would never cross again.

If the thought pained her, that, too, would be temporary. Wouldn't it?

Tyler clasped his hands together behind him, bowed his head and worked hard at not grinning like an idiot. It took considerable effort, surprising effort. He'd have danced down that street if he could have explained the impulse, but just why he felt so happy all of sudden remained something of a mystery.

Yes, he had enjoyed that kiss—reveled in it, honestly—but he had rarely done anything so foolish. He didn't know quite why he'd done it, really. Maybe he'd just wanted to prove to himself, or her, or both of them, that what she'd said was true, that she really hadn't loved Jerry Moody. But what was the point in that? It didn't change anything.

He'd had some half-formed notion of offering her a job, thereby tempting her into his orbit, but that, he now realized, was insanity. The differences between him and Charlotte were stark, insurmountable, and even if they weren't, she had no intention of ever leaving Eden—witness poor old Jerry still pining after her despite a wife and two children. Tyler suddenly felt rather sorry for the big goof.

Obviously Jerry had needed to look elsewhere to earn a living; Tyler could understand that. He couldn't imagine how anyone might stay here for any real length of time. The place didn't even offer a decent Internet connection, to say nothing of cell service. Even with those things, Tyler mused, failing to realize that *he* had replaced *anyone* in his own mind, he could never trust his family long enough to stay out of pocket for more than a week or two.

The pity of it was that he and Charlotte simply had no real time to get to know one another. Anything beyond that remained out of the question. Besides, if they didn't have enough against them, religion might well be an issue, too, at least for her. He didn't know what she meant by grace. Spiritual things had never figured very large in his life. He had nothing against faith, of course, it just didn't seem to apply to him.

She was right. He shouldn't have kissed her. Yet he couldn't regret it.

No woman had ever moved him like sweet, simple, unassuming Charlotte Jefford.

He thought about it as they hurried back toward the motel, the mist blowing in from the north quickening their footsteps.

She might fit him personally, but his world simply did not fit her. He couldn't imagine her doing the things his mother and sister did, sitting on charity boards and orchestrating formal dinner parties, worrying about making the proper fashion statement. Unlike Cassandra, Charlotte had no career ambitions, and she would never be content just spending money or filling her days with trips to the spa. Why, the women in his family would eat her alive.

Between Cassandra's sniffing put-downs and his mother's pointed commiseration, Charlotte wouldn't have a chance. Cassandra would murmur that Charlotte looked like a walking trash heap, her standard criticism for anyone who didn't dress to her specifications. She'd slyly attack Charlotte's education and her antecedents. His mother would simply heap pity on the poor woman until she suffocated.

He didn't even want to think about Shasta. His stepmother had been a nobody, a lowly secretary without connections or wealth, as his mother and sister all too often pointed out, before Comstock Aldrich had married her. Tyler had found, however, that the worst snobs were those who had the least about which to be snobbish. Shasta wouldn't stop at just turning up her nose at someone like Charlotte. She'd do her best to wound.

No sense fooling himself. Not one person in his life would understand what he saw in Charlotte, not even his brother, and they would undoubtedly make both their lives miserable if he should be so foolish as to try to forge some sort of relationship with her, though what that could be with a girl like Charlotte he couldn't imagine. She would expect nothing less than marriage, and that could never be for obvious reasons.

"Are you hungry?" she asked as they hurried around the back wing of the motel.

He wasn't, but he curled up his lips and nodded anyway.

"We'd better get in there before they eat it all, then," she told him, picking up the pace.

They ran the last little way, raindrops beginning to pelt them. Tyler laughed, feeling grand in spite of everything, and told himself that he deserved this vacation from his life.

He needed the renewal that he'd found here, and he was going to take it. Beyond that... He didn't want to think beyond that. For once, for a little while, he just wanted to be happy.

Charlotte folded the dish towel and draped it over the handle on the front of the oven. Behind her, Tyler closed the cabinet door. With the last dish now safely stowed away, she reached around to untie her apron, while Ty leaned a hip against the counter.

"Thanks for your help," she said, lifting the apron off over her head. Her braid flopped against her shoulder. She reached up and pushed it away, catching the glimmer of a smile as Tyler bowed his head. "What?"

He folded his arms. "You feed me. Again. Then you thank me for drying a few dishes. Seems to me you've got it backward."

Charlotte waved a hand dismissively. "I have to cook. You have to eat. It's just logical."

"It's generous," he corrected, "and I thank you." Leaning in slightly, he added, "Another excellent meal, by the way."

She inclined her head. "You're welcome. But you're putting too fine an edge on it. You've been lots of help around here these past few days. I'd be less than gracious to begrudge you a few meals."

In truth, he'd been more than simply helpful. Not only had he lent a hand with her chores, he'd entertained Hap at the dominoes table, offered Stu Booker, the local grocer and son of Hap's friend

Teddy, a line of private-label goods at rock-bottom prices, counseled Justus Inman on setting up a trust to protect the Inman family farm, befriended everyone else with whom he'd come in contact and followed around her brothers like a lost puppy.

His behavior puzzled her. Maybe he'd simply become bored, but that didn't explain why an accomplished, successful man like him continued to hang around little old Eden in the first place. He'd stopped that first night only because he couldn't find fuel for his car, but what kept him here?

After he'd kissed her she'd feared that she might be the reason why he continued hanging around, but now she thought that perhaps God was using this time to bring Ty closer to Him. A man with Tyler's resources could do much good for the kingdom of God, much good indeed.

Besides, it didn't make any sense for Ty to stay for her. He had to know as well as she did that the two of them did not suit each other. He lived in Dallas and would no doubt return there, but she would only leave Eden if God told her to, and she couldn't believe that would ever happen. Hap and her brothers needed her. That hadn't changed, nor would it.

Clearly that kiss had been a fluke, an aberration born of pity, if nothing else, and though it hurt a bit to think so, she could only conclude that it had shown Tyler in no uncertain terms that they could never have anything serious between them. For one thing, the kiss had not been repeated, which was just as it should be.

Still, the longer Tyler Aldrich lingered in Eden, the more she wondered why.

After expressing interest in the oil business on Sunday evening, Tyler had tagged along with Holt on Monday, returning that evening bedraggled and filthy in his cheap jeans and T-shirt. Despite the exhaustion stamped on his face, he'd seemed quite satisfied with himself, and Holt had grudgingly allowed that Tyler wasn't afraid of hard work. The conversation around the dinner table that night had demonstrated a fresh, incisive understanding on Ty's behalf of the laborious process of extracting crude oil from the ground.

After that experience, she shouldn't have been surprised when Ryan had shown up at her breakfast table on Tuesday morning, especially since he and Tyler had spoken on Sunday about the possibility of Ty's checking out the weight room at the high school. After downing three eggs, twice that many slices of bacon and half a pot of coffee, Ryan had left again, a casually dressed Tyler with him.

They'd returned at lunchtime, grinning and joking like little boys. The talk around the table then had been all about workout techniques and sports. Ryan had pronounced Ty good company as he'd taken his leave and headed back to the school, leaving Charlotte to shake her head in his wake.

On Tuesday afternoon and for all of Wednesday

Tyler had devoted himself to helping her, and she could truthfully concur with the assessments of both of her brothers. The man did not quail at getting his hands dirty, and his quick wit and pleasant manner made working with him pure fun, especially since his understanding of routine housekeeping proved laughably basic at best.

He'd quickly caught on, however, and had exhibited such rapt attention in the laundry room that she'd invited him to do his own washing. The pride he'd taken in that stack of fresh, clean clothing still made her smile.

"Listen," he said, breaking into her reverie, "now that everything's done, I was thinking about taking in a movie."

"Ah," she said, shifting mental gears. "In that case, you'll want to head up to Duncan again. You remember where the discount store is? The theater is about a half mile farther up 81 from there. It's on the same side of the road. You can't miss it."

His teeth flashed white before he glanced away. "Yes. I see. Well, how about a little TV instead? I have a couple of videos, but if those don't appeal to you we ought to be able to find something on broadcast, don't you think?"

We. She bit her lip, realizing too late that he'd been issuing an invitation, not asking directions. "I—I really don't know. I never watch television on Wednesday evening."

He cocked his head, and though his posture did

not change, she sensed a sudden tension in him. "No? Is there something else you usually do then?" His casual tone did nothing to dispel the heightened sense of interest.

"I—I usually attend the midweek prayer service at church."

"Oh." The awkwardness evaporated as quickly as it had developed. "Mind if I tag along?"

Mind? She tamped down a spurt of delight, reminding herself that his interest had nothing to do with her personally. His curiosity obviously knew no bounds, and he'd probably only invited her to watch television with him in the first place because he felt bored. Besides, no matter what kept Tyler here, she must remember that he would be leaving, probably sooner rather than later.

Becoming too attached to him, too used to his presence, too pleased by his attention would only cause her grief later. Nevertheless, no harm ever came from spending an hour in prayer with someone. She formed a polite, fond smile. "Let me get my things."

Chapter Eleven

Tyler looked around the circle of smiling faces, smoothed his damp palms on his jeaned thighs and tried not to fidget in his folding chair. He'd expected something similar to the Sunday service when he'd invited himself along with Charlotte, and things *had* started out that way. They'd congregated in the sanctuary, sung a few songs, listened to a few announcements—mostly prayer requests for those not in attendance—and then, to his shock, filed out to the fellowship hall where they'd broken into groups.

It had never occurred to Tyler that he could find himself sitting in a circle of strangers who were waiting for him to add his private concerns to their prayer lists. He glanced around the large room at the other circles. One, composed entirely of men, included both Holt and Ryan. They had waved and nodded but had not invited him to join them, no doubt knowing full well that he preferred to spend whatever time he had left here with their sister.

On Monday Holt had boldly asked him if he had any interest in Charlotte, to which Ty had replied, "For all the good that's likely to do me." Holt had grunted at that and lobbed a three-foot-long wrench at him so he could couple one pipe to another.

Ryan had been less direct but more obvious, blabbing incessantly about what a treasure Charlotte was and how they feared she would never find someone to truly appreciate her. Tyler had kept his own mouth shut, but he couldn't doubt that Ryan would give his blessing if Ty so much as hinted at wanting to pursue a relationship with Charlotte. Again, for all the good that would do him.

The participants of one of the other circles had already bowed their heads. A third group linked hands even as Tyler watched. Swiftly he turned back to his own circle, acutely aware of Charlotte sitting to his right and his lack of an answer for a personal prayer request.

"I, um… Well, I really don't have anything."

"We all have something that we need to take to God," an elderly woman noted kindly.

Tyler shifted his weight on the hard chair, feeling out of his depth. Charlotte, thankfully, came to his rescue.

"I think what Tyler means is that he wants his request to remain unspoken."

Unspoken. He remembered something about an unspoken request among those that the pastor had read from the pulpit earlier. That had seemed odd to him, but now he cravenly made the claim for himself. "Right. Un-unspoken."

Attention shifted to the person to Tyler's left, who went on at some length about the travails of his mother who was confined to a hospital. More to keep from looking at Charlotte than in real concern, Tyler focused his concentration on what the fellow had to say.

He couldn't help contrasting the poor old woman's situation with his father's. A private suite, personal nurses, limitless funds and doctors who fell all over themselves to provide the latest in treatment and technologies could not compare with crowded, shared rooms, noisy visitors, unresponsive, overworked staff, compassionate but helpless physicians and devoted families frustrated by uncaring and inadequate insurance bureaucracies.

It didn't seem fair that one experience should be better than another in the face of illness. Guilt clouded Tyler's mood until the man began to speak about his mother's sweet nature and happy spirit. Gradually guilt turned to envy, an emotion Tyler had little experience with and even less right to.

His had been a privileged existence, even if his father had been critical and distant and his mother self-absorbed. Yet he found himself coveting the obviously loving relationship that man had with his ailing mother. Uncomfortably self-conscious now, Tyler wished that he had not come.

That feeling only intensified as the group linked hands and bowed their heads. Instead of one person leading the entire group, each individual was expected to pray aloud, squeezing the hand of the person to his or her left when finished so that the prayer could continue around the circle uninterrupted. A middle-aged woman with salt-and-pepper hair across the way from Tyler began.

"Sovereign Lord God, You have told us that where we gather in Your name, You are there also. Thank You for coming to meet us, Father, as we approach Your throne in the name of Your Holy Son…"

As she spoke, Tyler felt an unusual sensation, as if something brushed against his skin, all of his skin at the same time. Later, as others took their turns, Tyler felt a movement inside his chest, a spreading almost, as though something tightly knotted unfurled. He didn't know what to call it, but he knew that he had never felt it before.

When Charlotte began to pray aloud, her voice a soft, gentle salve to his jangling senses, he perceived a presence, as if someone stood just behind him. This so unnerved him that he concentrated with fierce determination on Charlotte's words.

"We praise You, Lord, and thank You for Your many blessings," she was saying, "but then You know our needs even better than we do. You know that Granddad's arthritis pains him more and more lately. He never complains, but I dread the coming winter for him. Please ease his discomfort and don't let the cold rob him of enjoyment. Make me a blessing to him, as You have made him a blessing to me, and show us always what You would have us do."

She paused, and Tyler waited in an agony of dread for the squeeze on his hand that would make it his turn to speak. Instead, warmth spread from his palm, up his arm and throughout his body as she went on.

"Thank You, too, for Ty. He's been such help and he's brought such enjoyment. You know his needs, Lord, better than I do, even better than he does. I just lift those up to You, heavenly Father, trusting You to fill each and every one. Bless him. Bring him peace and joy."

When that dreaded squeeze finally came, Tyler couldn't have spoken if his life had depended on it. His heart seemed to have swollen inside his chest to the point that it crowded his throat. He couldn't shake the sudden conviction that he didn't deserve the gratitude Charlotte had expressed, but what could he say to that? What could he say, period? He knew a moment of agonizing uncertainty; yet, in that same moment, a voice seemed to whisper inside his mind, and suddenly the words just flowed from his mouth.

"We are blessed whether we deserve it or not, even when we aren't smart enough to ask for it. Thank You for that. A-and—"

His mind stuttered to a stop, suddenly blank. He shifted forward, and a calming hand settled upon his shoulder, bringing clarity and ease. His first thought was that it must be one of Charlotte's brothers, come to offer support.

Apparently he hadn't fooled them one bit. He'd wanted them to think that he was just like them, that he had experienced everything they had experienced, but he'd never participated in anything like this. He didn't have closely held religious beliefs as they did, but it didn't seem to matter at all. He felt deep gratitude just then for the kindness of the Jefford family.

They had taught him so much, more than he'd even realized until just that moment. Because of them, he saw what his own family lacked. Because of them, he understood that money and position didn't matter and true happiness came from within. Because of them, he knew that God was real. He'd always believed that on some level, but now he *knew,* and for the first time he really believed that he could actually talk to God, one-on-one.

Smiling inwardly, Tyler let his chin touch his chest and spoke from his heart. "Thank You for bringing me here to Eden. Thank You for new friends and good fun, for relaxation and broadening experiences, for renewal and…just…thank You." Something unexpected touched his mind, and he blurted it without thought. "Be with my family. We all need Your blessings even if we don't know it."

He started to say, "Amen," but remembered just

in time and squeezed the hand of the fellow next to him instead. For a moment silence filled the room, and then Tyler became aware of Holt's voice from across the hall.

"We bow to Your leadership, Lord, seeking to do Your will and knowing that You alone can provide wisdom and joy in our lives. We are Your creatures, Your children. Make us men You are proud to call Your own."

Not Holt, then, Tyler thought, though whoever had been behind him appeared to have silently moved off now. The fellow next to Tyler began to speak, but Holt's words seemed to have caught in Tyler's mind.

Make us men You are proud to call Your own.

With stabbing dismay, Tyler realized that he had not always been such a man. In fact, he did not really even know how to be such a man. Troubled, he mentally added a new prayer to those spoken in the circle.

Make me a man You are proud to call Your own.

The service moved back into the sanctuary. Tyler felt a warmth, an ease that he had not felt earlier. The smiles of those around him seemed softer, their laughter brighter, conversation more serene. Grover thanked everyone for coming, read a verse of Scripture, spoke a final prayer over the gathering and let the service close with a hymn.

Tyler did not catch the chapter and verse of the Scripture, but the words settled inside him.

"Therefore I say to you, all things for which you

pray and ask, believe that you have received them, and they shall be granted you."

Could it really be so simple? he wondered. Was it truly just a matter of belief?

Obviously, he mused, Charlotte's faith and that of her brothers and grandfather meant more than he'd assumed. But what did it mean for him?

He looked across the room to where Holt stood shaking hands with a gentleman so elderly that his frail body seemed to curl inward over the cane against which he balanced his slight weight. Their mutual affection lit the building. Ryan, meanwhile, laughed with a fortyish couple and Charlotte hugged a middle-aged woman with tightly curled hair.

Tyler had thought these people poor. He saw no designer suit in the place, no expensive watch, no artificial beauty, but he knew that no one here was poor. They were rich in spirit, far richer than he, in fact.

Perhaps their bank balances would not impress anyone, but what did that matter? No doubt they had their own troubles, their own concerns, perhaps even secrets that would shock their friends, but they were better off in many ways than the people he knew.

He found it disconcerting, to say the least, to realize that he might well be the poorest person in the building. Any unimportant claims to wealth that he could make had come to him purely through an accident of birth. These people had found their riches in a place where he had never before thought to look. They had found their wealth in their families and friends and their faith in God.

He looked to Charlotte's brothers again. A man's man, as strong and tough as they came, Holt also had brains and an indomitable will balanced by an honest spirit. Holt had everything it took to it make in Tyler's world, but when Tyler had said as much the other day, Holt had merely laughed.

"Been there, done that," he'd said. "Won't be going there again." He'd stopped what he'd been doing then and stood tall, legs braced wide apart, dirty, gloved hands at his sides. "I am where I belong," he'd added, no shred of doubt in his voice.

At the time, Tyler had thought he, too, knew where he belonged. Now he wondered.

He thought of Hap, the single most loving individual whom Ty had ever known. Being loving hadn't seemed much like a manly attribute to Tyler until the last few days, but Hap could show him just how it should be done.

Ryan, on the other hand, might be the happiest person Tyler knew. He bore the weight of his responsibilities with delight and facility, sincerity shining from his every pore. He loved his job and his family, his students and his teams, his town and his life. Not only could Ryan succeed in Tyler's world, he could succeed in a big way, but Tyler hadn't even bothered to say as much. He'd learned his lesson with Holt.

Or had he? He sensed that he still had lessons to learn here in Eden, Oklahoma. Important lessons.

Such thoughts occupied his mind as the meeting dispersed and he escorted Charlotte to his car. Only as he reached down to open the door for her did he ask the question that had been bothering him for some time.

"Who was that behind us in the prayer circle?" Someone had noticed his distress and calmed him with a touch. He owed that person a debt of thanks. It hadn't been Holt, but it might have been Ryan. Or perhaps the pastor?

Charlotte paused with one foot in the car and one foot out. She turned a puzzled look on him. "I don't know who you mean."

"There was someone standing just outside the circle, someone right behind us."

She thought a moment. He could see her mentally placing everyone present. Finally, she shook her head. "No, I don't think so."

"He put his hand on my shoulder," Tyler insisted, but she simply stared. "Ryan, maybe. Or Grover?"

"No, I saw them both with the men's group. I'd have known if either had risen."

Tyler frowned. "Well, someone put his hand on my shoulder."

She bit her lip, then a smile tugged it free again. Shrugging delicately, she dropped down into the seat. Tyler closed her inside and moved around the vehicle, his mind awhirl.

This place and these people suddenly had him questioning everything, especially himself.

* * *

"You did not!" Charlotte exclaimed, sure he was teasing.

The afternoon had turned fair and bright, hinting at a beautiful weekend, although the sunshine seemed fragile, almost crystalline, as if a sharp breeze might shatter it. Should Friday hold the same promise, she might start to believe and plan something frivolous like a final picnic before winter settled in. Sitting here on the patio with Tyler, sipping coffee and talking about youthful escapades, anything felt possible, anything at all.

"I did," Tyler admitted sheepishly, "I totaled the car leaving the dealership."

"What did your father do about that?" she asked, remembering that a broken window at the age of ten had resulted in a year at boarding school for Tyler. She prepared to sympathize, but Ty shrugged.

"Bought me another one."

Charlotte let her jaw drop. "No boarding school?"

"Not even a scolding."

She sagged, at a complete loss to understand. "That makes no sense whatsoever."

Ty spread his hands. "It seemed to at the time. I had a driver's license, so I had to have a car. Besides, by that age I was no bother to them any longer."

"I'd call wrecking a brand-new car a bother."

"Problems that could be fixed with money were not problems to my parents," Tyler pointed out. He lifted a hand to his temple, confessing, "The fact is, I got pretty wild there for a while, but as long as it didn't particularly disturb their lives they didn't seem to mind. Even after I graduated college and my father brought me into the company, so long as I showed up and took care of business, that was all that mattered." He went on to explain that he'd come into his trust fund by then and so had his own money.

Charlotte shook her head. "I'll hope you'll pardon me for saying so, but I'm amazed you turned out so well."

He flashed her a grin. "So you think I turned out okay, do you?"

Charlotte rolled her eyes. "Obviously."

"I don't know sometimes," he said with jarring honesty. "I think I was mostly trying to get their attention back then. Eventually I realized that my father respected just one thing, though, and I won his regard in that, at least. I think."

"Business," she surmised.

Nodding, he looked up into the sunlight. "I'm just not sure business acumen is all that should be passed from one generation to the next."

"Oh, I'm sure you'll do better with your own children," she said with sincerity, ignoring the foolish little pang that accompanied the thought.

Tyler stretched out on the chaise and crossed his ankles. "I'm not sure I'll ever have children," he told her.

"But of course you will."

"Will you, do you think?" he asked lightly.

For a moment she couldn't breathe, but then she remembered that regret and longing belied her faith. She had trusted God long ago to see to her future, and she'd accepted that the gifts she had in her grandfather and brothers surpassed any she could imagine for herself. What would she have done after the deaths of her parents without Hap and Holt and Ryan?

"These things are in God's hands," she said, "and capable hands they are."

The unmistakable sound of a car turning off the highway reached her ears, but she ignored it. Hap would take care of whoever had stopped in—guest, salesman or passerby seeking directions.

"I had a wreck once," she said, launching into the story.

Like Holt, her father had always run a few head of cattle on their place, and one day returning from town with a girlfriend of hers, they'd discovered a cow had gotten out and gone wandering around the yard. Her father had left the truck idling while he'd gone on foot to drive the cow back into the pasture. Charlotte, all of twelve, had decided to pull the truck up to the house. She'd been driving around the ranch for years, but her friend, who lived in town and hadn't known that, had panicked as soon as the truck started moving. She'd grabbed hold of Charlotte and tried to hide her face against Charlotte's shoulder.

"All I could see was black hair," Charlotte recalled with a chortle. "I tried to stomp the break but kept hitting the clutch. It didn't seem like I'd driven ten feet, but it had to be more like ten yards."

"What finally stopped you?" he asked, chuckling.

"The barn."

"It's a miracle you weren't killed!"

"You're telling me. I had to drive right past the propane tank to get there."

Hap rounded the corner of the building just then, saying, "Here they are. Ty, you got company, son."

Tyler twisted around in his seat just as a tall, slender, elegantly attired blonde walked into view. Charlotte sat up a little straighter, suddenly conscious of her shaggy sweater, rumpled shirt, faded jeans and run-down sneakers. Hoping that the hole in her left sock didn't show, she crossed her ankles primly, not that it helped anything.

The blonde might have walked straight out of the pages of a fashion magazine. The slender skirt of her moss-green suit emphasized the svelte length of her legs, while the short, belted jacket and the filmy silk blouse beneath it called attention to the feminine lushness of her figure. Her pale hair had been twisted into a sleek, sophisticated knot that could not have been accomplished without expertise while the pearls at her earlobes and the diamond at her throat fairly shouted wealth.

Charlotte's stomach dropped to the rubber-clad

soles of her feet while Tyler literally groaned. The blonde folded her arms, one foot swinging out to the side in an obviously practiced pose.

"Ty?" she queried, making that single syllable sound like an indictment as well as irony. Abruptly, her focus switched to Charlotte, her subtly made-up eyes narrowing.

Tyler sighed and asked, "How did you find me?"

"If you don't want to be found, you shouldn't use your company credit card," the blonde retorted.

Ty winced. Charlotte remembered how often he'd used that card during the past few days. He'd been shopping with that card, and last night after prayer meeting he'd driven Charlotte all the way to Waurika for malts. Just this morning he'd insisted on paying his bill with it so Hap could balance the accounts. He'd remarked repeatedly that he really needed to get some cash because not everyone around here took plastic.

Somehow, though, Charlotte didn't think the credit card was the problem. The problem stood in front of them. Who was this woman? Employee? Coworker? Girlfriend?

Charlotte couldn't bear to think the latter, but the possibility could not be ignored, not with this cool blonde standing here alternately smirking and glaring at her.

Ty bowed his head, pressing thumb and fingers to his temples. Then he looked up and smiled wanly at Charlotte.

"Sorry. I haven't introduced my sister."

Sister! Charlotte felt an instant of relief, followed swiftly by dismay, which she attempted to hide with a bright smile. If Tyler's sister represented the kind of woman who moved in Tyler's world, and she no doubt did, then Charlotte could never expect to meet his standards. Only then did she realize that on some level she had hoped to do just that.

Tyler stood, indicating his sister with a wave of his hand. "Cassandra Aldrich." He looked to her and placed a hand on the back of Charlotte's chair. "Allow me to introduce my hostess, Charlotte Jefford. You've already met her grandfather, Hap."

"Charlotte," Cassandra parroted with a little smirk, her gaze sweeping over Charlotte again. "What an old-fashioned name." Tyler's shoe scraped on the patio paving, and she quickly corrected herself, smile broadening. "Classic, I should've said. My own is a classic name. Tell me, do they call you Lottie? Now *that* would be old-fashioned."

"Cut it out, Cassandra."

"Whatever do you mean, *Ty?*"

"You know exactly what I mean."

Cassandra laughed. The sound contained nothing of amusement or pleasure. "It's a little hang-up of our mother's," she said to Charlotte. "She can't abide sobriquets. That means nicknames, by the way."

"I know what it means," Charlotte informed her quietly.

If she had needed proof that she would not fit into Tyler's world, she now had it in spades, not that she had been considering any such thing. Had she? No, of course not. She knew where she belonged. When had she started to second-guess that?

"What are you doing here, Cassandra?" Tyler asked coldly.

An unpleasant expression tightened Cassandra's pink mouth. "Perhaps little Lottie and her grandpa will excuse us while we discuss it."

"That's enough!" Tyler ordered, but Charlotte quickly leaped to her feet and brushed past him.

"Come on, Granddad, I need you to watch the front desk while I start dinner."

"Charlotte, don't—" Tyler began.

"No, really, it's fine," she told him, smiling to forestall further objection. "I'll see you later?"

"Yes, of course, but—"

Ducking her head, she hurried on by him, determined not to cry. It would be stupid to cry about Cassandra Aldrich's petty cruelties, and she wouldn't think of crying for any other reason. That would be beyond foolish.

Catching Hap by the arm, she turned him away from the unpleasant scene. They made it around the corner before Hap grumbled, "Not a good thing, her showing up like that."

Not a good thing at all, Charlotte thought, but she said nothing. The lump in her throat would not permit it.

She set about preparing the evening meal at once, but even as she worked, her thoughts were with Tyler and his sister. He would leave now. She knew it.

She'd always known he would go away again, had expected every day to be his last with them. Somehow, though, she had not been prepared for her own disappointment.

Tyler Aldrich, she realized suddenly, would leave a huge gaping hole in her life when he left.

How that could be after so short a time, she simply did not know.

Chapter Twelve

"That was a nasty thing to do," Tyler hissed.

Cassandra rolled her eyes. "Oh, please. Don't tell me that Little Miss Lumberjack and Old Man Overalls are your new best friends."

"Those people have been very good to me."

"Well, duh." She cast a spurious glance toward the rooms. "You can bet it isn't every day they get an Aldrich in here."

"It doesn't have anything to do with that," Tyler vowed.

"Right. Like you really believe that."

Suddenly weary, he dropped down onto the chaise again. Sniffing, Cassandra maneuvered herself in front of a lawn chair but didn't sit. Tyler reflected glumly that this one outfit of Cassandra's probably cost more than Charlotte's entire wardrobe.

"What do you want, Cassandra?"

She folded her arms in that patented display of contempt. "I want you to do your job."

He sat back and crossed his legs. "That's what I've been doing."

She lifted her eyebrows at the jeans he wore but stayed on topic. "Sure you have. That's why no one's heard from you in a week. What did you do, turn off your phone?"

"Yes."

"Typically juvenile."

He didn't deny it. Why should he bother defending himself? Cassandra would never understand, and what difference did it make that the cell service was spotty at best?

"Do you want to criticize, or do you want to tell me why you bothered to drive all this way?"

Clearly, she hated to say what had brought her here. Whatever it was literally made her grit her teeth. In the end, though, she had no choice. One of their major suppliers had gotten hit by Immigration. They'd lost so much staff that they'd effectively been shut down.

"We have to do something," she insisted. "Quick. Or by next week we won't be able to stock our shelves."

Tyler frowned. He should have anticipated something like this. The company policy forbade dealing with domestic producers who employed illegal immigrants, but realistically even lip service took a backseat to cost. "Who is it?"

"Paxit."

Tyler's frown deepened. It would have to be their largest supplier. By coincidence, the Paxit corporate offices were in Lewisville, Texas, on the far northern edge of the greater Dallas Metroplex.

"What is the board recommending?"

Cassandra snorted. "The board recommends pointing fingers and hanging each other out to dry, as usual. Shasta is threatening to sue someone, anyone. Preston blames you for continuing Father's policies."

Tyler shook his head. "That's novel. He usually blames me for making too many changes."

"You should have been there to handle this!" Cassandra accused, going from cynical to white-hot in the blink of an eye. She shared that trait with their late father. When all else failed, resort to anger. It didn't help that this time she happened to be right. "Mother has taken to her bed, sure we'll all be bankrupt in a week," she added petulantly.

Tyler sighed. While their father had resorted to towering rage, Amanda Aldrich routinely broke down in weeping self-pity punctuated with threats of impending "nervous breakdowns," which the family tended to ignore, as her husband had done.

"I've talked to Spencer-Hatten," Cassandra announced, lifting her chin defiantly. "The price is steep, and there's no time to relabel, but at least we could keep the shelves filled with SH goods."

"Except that the board won't go along with

that," Tyler said flatly, "because Spencer-Hatten will demand a seat, and the next thing we know they'll own us."

Her chin went up another notch. "You don't know that."

He did know it, and so did Cassandra, but she'd rather see him fail than preserve the family business. No doubt she'd cut some sort of personal deal with Spencer-Hatten. He expected nothing less.

Tyler sighed inwardly. He had been foolish and self-indulgent. Perhaps he could have justified staying over the weekend, but what excuse did he have for remaining throughout the week? The time had come to return to his life.

The thought depressed him, but he had a job to do, the job for which he had been bred and groomed his entire life. He would be better at that job now; he had no doubt. Although at the moment he didn't have the faintest notion how he would solve this problem, he knew that he would find a way.

The prayer that had whispered through his mind last night came to him again. *Make me a man You are proud to call Your own.* He intentionally added another line. *Guide me in this.*

Tilting back his head, he looked up at his sister. Her cold, steely beauty, underlaid with the bitterness of resentment, cut his heart like a knife. Suddenly he longed to take her in his arms and tell her that all would be well. It's what Holt or Ryan would have done for their sister. *His* sister would probably come out swinging if he did such a thing, provided the shock didn't kill her first.

Sorrow draped him like a shroud. He pushed it aside and rose to his feet. "Go home, Cassandra. Tell the board we'll be meeting for lunch tomorrow. Then call the caterer."

Her eyes and lips narrowed cynically. "Haute cuisine won't get you out of this one, little brother."

God will, he thought, *if I ask Him.* And he intended to do just that. Charlotte would show him how. It might be the very last thing they would ever do together, but what could be more fitting?

Cassandra pivoted on her very narrow heel and sauntered away without another word. Tyler stood where she'd left him, head bowed, until he heard a door close and the car drive away. Sucking in a deep, calming breath, he went in search of Charlotte. As expected, he found her in the kitchen, a knife in hand as she sliced carrots.

"I'm sorry," he said. "Cassandra was out of line. She usually is."

Charlotte shook her head, her bright braid swinging between her shoulder blades. He'd never told her how much he liked her hair loose. He never would now. What possible purpose could it serve except to make leaving all the more difficult?

"Don't be silly," she said. "I'd never let anything like a little nickname offend me."

"I know you wouldn't, but she intended to offend."

Charlotte turned a smile in his direction, such softness in her eyes that his heart broke. "That's not your fault."

He couldn't look into those lovely eyes any longer. It hurt too much, as did what he had to say next. "I'll be leaving early in the morning."

She turned away, her hands still on the cutting board. "Not tonight?" she asked after a moment.

One more night, he thought. One more dinner. One more moment of ease and light. Not so easy now, not so light. Still, he would stay. For one more night.

"Tomorrow," he confirmed, "early. Tonight after dinner I'd appreciate it if you would pray with me."

He heard a clunk just before she whirled and came into his arms. Closing his eyes, he held her tight for a long, sweet moment.

"I wish it could be different," she whispered, "but you know it can't."

Ty swallowed. "I know. You have to stay in Eden."

"And you must return to your responsibilities," she said, pulling away to dab at her eyes. Now that the truth had been laid bare, they would pretend no longer. "We had fun, didn't we?"

He nodded but could not speak. She turned back to the cutting board.

"Would you set the table, please? The good china, I think." She shot him a bright smile that cut him to ribbons. "We'll end as we began."

It was all he could do to lift down the plates, one by one, without shattering his composure, if nothing else.

Dinner became a family affair. Hap must have called Ryan and Holt, the latter of whom dragged in filthy from a day in the field and spent long minutes washing until Charlotte deemed him clean enough to sit at her table.

Conversation could only be described as lively, if slightly forced. Everyone laughed and joked and talked at the same time. No one inquired about Cassandra or mentioned that Tyler would be leaving, and for that he silently thanked them.

After the meal, Hap's cronies began arriving, and Holt got up to take himself off home. He gave Tyler a hearty handshake and patted Charlotte's shoulder consolingly as he went out the door. Ryan hung around long enough to have a private word with Tyler.

"How often you reckon you'll be getting back up this way?"

Tyler had been beating himself with that question all evening. He could come every now and again, surely, but to what purpose? Why make himself and Charlotte miserable by projecting hope where none existed? Sick at heart, he could only say that he didn't know when he'd be back their way.

Ryan looked disappointed by that, but then he smiled and said, "Guess it's something else to pray about."

"Yes, it is," Tyler agreed solemnly, "and I'd appreciate it if you'd do just that."

"I absolutely will," Ryan said, grasping Ty's hand warmly. "Just know that whenever you come back, you'll be welcome."

Ty had to clear his throat. "Thank you, Ryan."

With a wary look in Charlotte's direction, Ryan left to attend one of his usual school functions. By that time Hap had migrated to the lobby for his usual game of dominoes. Tyler insisted on helping Charlotte finish cleaning up.

They worked in silence, broken only by the clink of dishes and the creak of cabinet doors. Eventually nothing remained to do. Charlotte removed her apron and looked at him.

"You said you wanted to pray."

Tyler wondered if he could manage that now, and he felt a little foolish for even bringing it up. "Oh, that. It's a business thing. I shouldn't have bothered you with it."

Ignoring that, she led him back to the table. They sat down again and linked hands. He explained the situation. Her prayer surprised him. She asked for wisdom for him in figuring out how to deal with the matter, but then she asked God to give him wisdom in dealing with his family, especially his sister.

"Just help them show each other how important they are to one another."

She squeezed his hand then, but she'd given him so much to think about that his mind whirled. He could barely form a sentence. Finally he came up with, "I guess that's it in a nutshell, God. I need wisdom to deal with all of this, and I don't think I even realized that until now, so maybe we've made a start. Thank You for that. Amen."

"Amen," Charlotte whispered.

They lifted their heads just as laughter exploded from the front room.

Charlotte rose, saying, "I don't know about you, but I think I need a little of that. Want to join me? Hap will understand if you'd rather not, but I know that the others would like to see you again."

One last time, she meant. One last time. Ty would rather have done anything than walk into that room and say his goodbyes—anything except walk through the door *without* saying them.

Joining the others turned out to be a wise decision. Hap, Teddy, Grover and Justus routinely kept each other and everyone around them in stitches, and they seemed especially jovial and clever that night. Tyler took their ribbing good-naturedly, knowing it for a sign of affection, and sat in for occasional hands while one or the other of them excused himself.

Eventually the game broke up. Grover left first, but not before giving Ty a personal farewell.

"We'll miss you, son. Have a safe trip and don't be a stranger now, you hear? I'll be praying for you."

"Thank you, sir."

"None of that now. You're all but family here."

More than family by Aldrich standards, Tyler reflected morosely. "Again, I thank you."

Teddy and Justus settled for handshakes and silent nods. As soon as they'd gone, Hap immediately attempted to make himself scarce, but Tyler wasn't about to let him get away with that. Clapping a hand on the old man's shoulder, he laughingly declared, "Oh, no, you don't."

Hap grimaced and hitched himself around. "I always hate goodbyes."

Tyler hated this one, but he gamely stuck out his hand. "It's been a pleasure. One I'll never forget. Grover said I was the next thing to family, but you've made me feel more like family than anyone else ever has. I needed that."

"Shucks, son," Hap said in a voice even rougher than usual. "If you're gonna do a thing, do it right." With that he engulfed Ty in a hug.

Clasping the old man carefully, Tyler felt his eyes mist. This was what a godly man should be, he thought.

Lord, make me a man You are proud to call Your own.

After delivering a bristly kiss to Tyler's cheek, Hap turned away, his stiff, shuffling steps carrying him into the apartment.

Tyler could not remember ever being kissed by another man, and suddenly he mourned the loss. What he would have given as a child for such a simple thing as that from his father. This time in Eden just seemed chock-full of surprising treasures, and the main one stood behind him.

He puffed out a breath and, when it could not be put off any longer, turned to Charlotte. She stood with her arms wrapped tightly about her middle, a clear warning that he heeded.

"I'll be heading out early," he said, "before daylight, even. I have an important lunch meeting, and I need to prepare."

She nodded. "You'll be careful going home? You won't drive too fast?"

Home? he thought. Funny, this place seemed more like home now than Dallas did, but he nodded.

"I guess this is goodbye, then," she said softly.

Again he nodded, but long seconds ticked by and still his feet did not move toward the door. "Charlotte," he began, surprising himself by moving forward rather than away. "I truly wish—"

She interrupted by simply stepping into his arms. "What is, is, Ty." She lifted her head, her eyes swimming with tears. "I'm glad to have known you, Tyler Aldrich. I'll be praying for you."

"I'm counting on that," he told her in a choked voice, then he got out of there before he did something stupid and they both broke down.

As he walked away, he told himself that it was time he started talking to God on a regular basis, and since there was no time like the present, he looked up at the black sky, whispering, "Lord, take care of her. Take care of them all. I know You will. They're good folks and they love You."

He'd learned a little something about that himself.

Charlotte passed a sleepless night, alternately praying and wondering if Tyler slept. Did he want to go back to his old life? she asked herself. Of course he did. Otherwise, he would not do it. Would he?

At other times she wondered if she might be wrong about God's will for her, but how could that be? Her family needed her, and she needed them. She remembered how very, very sure she had been before, when Jerry had insisted that the job waiting for him in Tulsa was their future.

"Your future," she had told him firmly. "Mine is here."

And it had been. It still was. It must be.

Besides, Tyler had not actually asked her to go with him. Surely he would have if he wanted that. Yet his going felt terribly like abandonment. She prayed for acceptance, remembering her happy life before Tyler Aldrich had found himself out of gas in Eden.

She would find that contentment again. Surely she would.

Long before daylight, Charlotte had her fill of these restless thoughts. Finally, she rose from her bed to throw on her robe and pad quietly into the kitchen to make up a pot of coffee. She worked in the dark, lest she awaken Hap. About halfway through the brewing process, she recognized the throaty rumble of Ty's car engine.

The sound drew her to open the kitchen door, but then she stood behind the screen to watch the sleek automobile back out of the covered space where it had spent the majority of the past week. Could it really be a mere week since she had first laid eyes on the man from Big D?

Only the screen and the dark stood between her and one final farewell. The car rolled forward, coming to rest just outside, not a dozen yards between them. Her hand reached out to push open the screen—but, no. If she went out there now, things might be said that shouldn't be.

The car rolled forward once more, a fortune on wheels, another world on wheels. She watched the turn signal blink, then the car swung out onto the highway heading south. In moments it had disappeared as if it had never existed.

Wiping her tears from her cheeks with the sleeve of her robe, she closed the door on this short but surprisingly poignant chapter in her life.

Chapter Thirteen

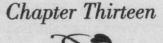

The solution came to Tyler as he crossed the Red River. One moment he was asking God to help him do what he knew he must, and the next moment the dilemma that pulled him back to Dallas had been reduced to a plan of action. He couldn't imagine why he hadn't thought of it at once.

Sure of the rightness of his plan, he drove straight to the corporate office of Paxit Distributing on the northern outskirts of the DFW Metroplex, where the owner and CEO, Comer Paxton, received him into his Spartan office with obvious dread and resignation. The fellow fully expected Tyler to cancel his contract, which had been Tyler's intention in the beginning. Now he had a better plan.

In a matter of a few hours, they hammered out a deal for Aldrich & Associates to buy Paxit Distributing and hire Paxton himself to run it. That would keep Paxit operational, allow it to settle the fines levied by the government, avoid any major rupture in the lines of supply and give Aldrich & Associates greater control over its own fate.

Getting the Aldrich board to sign off might take some doing, but Tyler knew it would work out when Comer Paxton gripped his hands together, bowed his head over them and exclaimed, "This is the answer to my prayers!"

"Funny you should say that," Tyler told him, smiling. "It's the answer to my prayers, too."

Over the next short while, he watched Comer Paxton come alive. Worry and defeat seemed to fall away; hope blossomed in the man's eyes. Corresponding gladness welled in Tyler. The sheer pleasure of finding a solution that protected this man's life's work and benefited everyone in the mix came as a surprise.

So this, Tyler thought, heading toward his own corporate offices, *is joy.* Funny that he should find it in the midst of dejection. He pushed that thought away, concentrating on business.

It did not, as Tyler had predicted, go smoothly with the board. Cassandra made an impassioned argument for Spencer-Hatten, and Shasta railed about the amount of money involved, but the numbers proved that Tyler's plan would not only guarantee an uninterrupted chain of supply, it would ultimately lead to substantial savings and growth.

Ty tried to listen to every side of every point of the debate, exercising patience he hadn't known he possessed. The arguing and the posturing endemic to his family continued as expected, but in the end even Cassandra voted in favor of Tyler's proposal, proof to his mind that Charlotte and the rest of the Jefford family were keeping him in their prayers.

Over that next weekend, thoughts of Charlotte and the others came to him constantly, and every time they did, he remembered the prayer that he had "caught" from Holt at the prayer meeting.

Lord, make me a man You are proud to call Your own.

He went to church on Sunday, realizing that being a man to make God proud required more than intention on his part. He couldn't just sit around waiting for God to create something in him that he did not actively pursue for himself. For the first time he became more than a mere observer. He really participated in the worship. He talked over things with God, too.

Still, something was missing. He kept thinking about that word *grace.* He mulled over the idea of talking to the pastor of his church about it, but he didn't even know how to broach the subject. If he could just talk to Hap then this confusion would leave him, but talking to Hap meant talking to Charlotte or, even worse, not talking to her, not seeing her. But wasn't that the case now?

He wondered if melancholy could kill a man.

Charlotte heard the creak of the screen door and quickly gulped back her tears, knowing that the night and the still, chilly air would amplify the smallest sound, even a sniff. Her brother's foot-steps—she'd know them anywhere—scraped against the pavement as he walked toward his truck, but then they shifted, and she knew she'd been found out.

She should have gone to bed. She'd meant to as soon as she'd told Hap and Holt that was where she was headed. Instead, she'd found herself sitting alone on the patio, steeped in self-pity. Grateful for the darkness of the shadow that sheltered her face from the stark revelation of the light at her back, she sat up a little straighter.

"What're you doing out here?" Holt asked, his shadow falling long and lean across the paving stones.

She tried to sound as if she hadn't been crying. "Just enjoying the peace and quiet."

Holt's shadow brought its hands to its hips. "You been crying over him."

"Him?" Her head bowed beneath the weight of pretense.

"What is it about Tyler Aldrich that's done this to you?" Holt demanded.

"I don't know," she answered softly, her voice wobbling.

"Well, it's not his money," Holt grumbled, "but just what it is I can't figure out."

She laughed mirthlessly, dashing tears from her eyes, and tried not to mentally run down a long list of what she liked about Tyler. "Actually, I'd like him a lot better without all that money."

Holt's feet scraped on the paving. "No, you wouldn't. It would just make it easier."

She shook her head, swallowing. "It's more than that. It's everything that goes with it."

"That could change," Holt said after a moment.

She dared not even contemplate the possibility. Instead, she calmed herself with the cold, hard truth. "I don't see how."

"You don't have to," Holt said harshly. Then his voice softened, though not without a touch of regret. "You ought to know that by now. We'll pray on it. All right?"

Stepping forward, he laid his big, work-roughened hand on her shoulder. Smiling, Charlotte trapped it against her cheek.

"All right."

On the second Wednesday evening in November, almost three weeks since he'd left Eden, Tyler stood looking out over the city at the distinctive Dallas skyline. He felt the emptiness of the apartment at his back. Sumptuous and far larger than a single man required, the Turtle Creek penthouse provided him with an upscale address, convenience and privacy, but in that moment he'd have gladly traded this place for a shabby little room with the furniture bolted to the wall, so long as that room was at the Heavenly Arms Motel.

Ty laid his forehead against the cool plate-glass window and spoke to God. "Help me here. I'm trying. I thought I knew what I was supposed to do, but now I'm just not sure."

He knew what he wanted to do. He wanted to go back to Eden and see Charlotte and Hap and Holt and Ryan, Grover and Teddy and Justus, too. Answers could be found there, he felt sure, but complications waited there, too.

"My feelings for Charlotte haven't gone away," he told God, "and it seems foolish to put myself into a situation where I can't expect anything but rejection and disappointment."

Leaving before had inflicted what had felt like a mortal wound, and it still ached. He suspected it always would. Lifting a hand, he pressed it against the center of his chest. His heart beat solidly against his palm, echoing into the hollowness inside him. Suddenly he knew that he didn't have anything to lose and everything to gain by returning to Eden.

Maybe he and Charlotte were not meant to be together, but the Jefford family had come into his life for a reason, and that reason had not yet been fully accomplished. Maybe his feelings for Charlotte were the price he paid for the work that God wanted to do in his life, and maybe he'd only now really opened himself up to what God wanted to do for him.

He took a deep breath and lifted his face to the night sky. Ambient light and pollution hid the stars, but that did not block the line of communication.

"All right," he said. "I'll go back if that's what

You want. If it's not, well, I'm sure You can find a way to make that clear to me."

For some time, he stood there, feeling small but peaceful.

Strange how he found the most peace in those moments when he felt the least like himself, the least like the Tyler Aldrich of old. That Tyler was someone "important." This Tyler, the one he'd started to think of as the real Tyler, was just another soul in the great universe that he'd recently heard described as God's footstool.

The thought humbled him, but maybe that needed to happen. He certainly liked this newly humbled Tyler better than the old "important" Tyler. No doubt God liked him better, too, but Ty suspected that he had a way to go before either he or God could actually be proud of him.

He left from the office on the following Friday morning. This time he let everyone know where he could be reached and when he'd be back. Cassandra followed him out, making snide remarks and probing for information and weak spots.

"You're actually going back to Podunksville?" she demanded, on the way to the elevator.

"The name of the town is Eden, Oklahoma."

"You're blowing off work again to play country bumpkin."

Ty smiled. "Guess I just have the soul of a small-town boy."

"It's that woman," she declared, folding her arms.

The elevator door slid open just then, and Tyler stepped inside, saying nothing. He pressed the button for the first sublevel where he and a few others parked. At the last moment, Cassandra slid into the elevator car with him.

"She's no one," Cassandra said tartly.

Tyler clamped his teeth against an angry retort. He had to swallow before he could point out, "You don't even know her."

"I know her type."

"You *think* you know her type."

"You're an Aldrich!" Cassandra exclaimed. The elevator set down just as Cassandra stomped her foot. "You just like being a big fish in a small pond," she accused, trailing him as he walked out into the parking basement. "You throw your money around, and they fawn and fall all over you, don't they?"

The very idea amused him because it couldn't have been further from the truth. "These people are my friends, Cassandra," he said, moving toward the car and unlocking it remotely.

"Oh, please. Friends are of your own class."

He paused in the act of opening the driver's door and turned on her. "Class? *Class?* What is this, the 1800s?"

"You know what I mean!"

"Unfortunately, I do," he said, yanking open the door and dropping down into the driver's seat. "But let me tell you something. Not only are those people my friends, I am honored by them."

He reflected bitterly that he'd hoped Cassandra might somehow become the kind of sister that Charlotte was to her brothers, then he realized suddenly that for that to happen, he first had to be the kind of brother that Holt and Ryan were. He tried to think how Holt or Ryan might take leave of their sister.

"See you on Monday," he said stiffly, and then, almost against his will, he added, "By the way, I love you, even if you are a terrible snob."

With that, he closed the door, started the engine and drove away, leaving her standing there with her mouth agape and a look of complete shock on her face.

He felt some surprise himself. He hadn't planned to tell her that he loved her; he hadn't even realized that he did until he'd said it. In fact, had anyone asked him if he loved his sister, he'd probably have responded with a lot of mumbo jumbo and qualifications meant to evade any real answer.

Perhaps it wouldn't change anything, but he was glad that he'd said it. The very act of saying that he loved his sister had somehow freed him to do so. After all these years of fussing and fighting, he actually loved his big sister, and he intended to do a better job of it in the future.

He thought about that as he drove north, noting idly the changes in the landscape. With Thanksgiving almost upon them, the trees stood denuded. Even the dull, light brown grass had been swept clean of leaves by the swirling breeze that grew increasingly sharp the farther that he traveled. This time, though, he'd come prepared.

What he had not done was call ahead. It had never even occurred to him. Many times over these past weeks he'd reached for the telephone, hungry just for the sound of Charlotte's voice, but then he'd told himself that it wouldn't be fair to either of them. Oddly, though, when he'd made the decision to return to Eden, he'd never even thought of calling.

Now he wondered if she would want him to come. Others had said he'd always be welcome, but Charlotte had not. For all he knew, she might not even be there. He'd thought of her as tied to the motel, but nothing said she couldn't leave for a few days. Maybe God didn't intend for him to see her.

Gulping, Tyler promised himself that he would take whatever came. If it turned out that he could only spend time with Hap, then he'd spend time with Hap and gladly.

By the time he pulled up beneath the drive-through at the motel, he could barely wait to leap from the car, but he forced himself to walk sedately up the ramp and push through the door into the lobby. Hap met him in the middle of the floor, laughing and holding open his arms.

"Ty!"

They engaged in a warm hug punctuated with enthusiastic back pounding. "How are you?"

"Better just seeing you here," Hap told him.

"You feeling okay? Arthritis bothering you?"

Hap waved that away. "How come you didn't let us know you was coming? We'd have called out the troops to greet you."

Ty just shrugged. "How is everyone?"

Hap grinned. "*Everyone's* missed you," he said slyly. "She's in there laying the lunch table right now."

Tyler looked to the apartment door. He hadn't fooled Hap one bit, but he couldn't have cared less. He smiled. "At least my timing's good. I made it for lunch."

"Go on," Hap instructed with a jerk of his head.

Nodding his appreciation, Ty moved forward. His heart pounded harder with every step. He opened the door without knocking. Charlotte paused and looked up, the plate in her hand hovering over the table.

Tyler's knees went weak; he wouldn't have been surprised to find himself facedown on the rug the next moment. Instead, he somehow managed to step forward. She all but dropped the plate, and then she sat down hard in the chair she'd pulled out to give her access to the entire table.

Before he'd taken the next step Tyler knew that he needed this woman like he needed air and food and drink. He decided right then that he was going to have her in his life one way or another, even if it meant giving up everything in Dallas and staying here with her. First, though, he had to convince her that they belonged together.

From the look on her face, he figured he had reason to hope.

Charlotte laughed. Her heart had stopped when she'd looked up to find Ty standing there, but as he crossed the room her happiness bubbled over. Thrilled to the soles of her feet, she popped up again and went to meet him, mentally thanking God.

Over these past weeks, she'd wondered and pondered. Had she limited God by dismissing the possibility that He might mean for her and Ty to find a way to join their lives? It could only work, of course, if they were both totally open to God's will. She'd been thinking, too, about Tyler's understanding of that. She had, in fact, spent a good deal of time praying about it. Now, however, everything pretty much flew right out of her head.

She was so happy she hardly knew what to do with herself. Too happy. For once, she didn't care.

"You're here!"

He held her at arm's length, grinning down at her. "And hungry. What's for lunch?"

She laughed, blinking back the tears that burned behind her eyes. The past three weeks seemed like a moment to her now. Oddly, they'd felt like an eternity at the time.

"Homemade chicken noodle soup and crackers," she told him.

"Sounds good. Can I help?"

"You'd better." Beaming, she caught his hand and led him toward the kitchen, silently praying.

Thank You, Lord, but oh, what does this mean?

Something told her that only time would tell. God was in charge here. She would let things play out as He dictated and be glad that Tyler hadn't forgotten them after all.

They spent an easy weekend, doing not much of anything. Holt and Hap went out for catfish that night, while Charlotte and Ty stayed in. Ryan joined them, having a rare Friday off during football season, for pizza that Ty had delivered all the way from Waurika.

Ty turned down the opportunity to work off the extra calories with Ryan at the school gym the next morning. Instead he helped Charlotte finish her chores early so they could meander around the park, talking over the changes he'd made at the company and in dealing with his family.

She applauded his solution to the problem that had called him back to Dallas and tried to reinforce his instincts about dealing with his family by pointing out that no one could change anyone else, only oneself.

"You can't control what they do or say, only how you react to it."

"I hadn't thought of it that way," he admitted, "but it makes stellar sense."

She ducked her head, pleased, and he slung an arm about her shoulders companionably. Excitement shimmered through her. How could it be possible, she wondered, to feel such exhilaration and such contentment in the very same moment? The feelings persisted all through the evening, which they spent with the family, talking and joking and playing dominoes with Hap and his friends.

They went to church together the next day, and she couldn't help noticing how raptly Ty paid attention to everything that was said and done. After dinner, he had a long talk with Hap in the front room while she and Holt and Ryan cleaned up. Normally, she'd have left it to her brothers, but Ty had asked for this time alone with her grandfather.

Later, Ty suggested another walk, and they set off for the park once more, though evening had already settled in and he'd made it clear that he would be heading back to Dallas soon.

"Mind if I ask what you and Granddad were talking about?" she ventured when it became apparent that he wasn't going to volunteer the information.

He tugged at his earlobe. "Ah, I just needed some things cleared up."

"Was he able to do that for you?"

"Not sure yet." Ty slanted a wry glance down at her. "I'll let you know when I am."

She chuckled and gave it up. "Okay, then."

They walked a little farther before she brought up something else that had been on her mind. This weekend had been fleeting, and perhaps any time they managed to spend together would be, but she could not bear the thought of never seeing him again. She'd mourned when he'd gone away before, and perhaps she would mourn like that again. Nothing had been settled between them, and perhaps nothing ever would be, but she just couldn't let him go without knowing when she'd see him again.

"I'd like you to come for Thanksgiving."

He stopped, and so did she, turning to face him. His hands skimmed down the length of her arms. "I'd be delighted."

She dipped her head, more pleased than she probably should have been. Nothing about this situation had changed, after all. Heartbreak undoubtedly waited down the road, but Thanksgiving would be sweet.

"I realize it means driving up here two weeks in a row."

"That's true," he agreed lightly. "Maybe I deserve some consideration for that."

She laughed. "Like what?"

Cupping her face in his hands, he tilted her face up to his. "I want you to pray about us."

"Us?" she echoed weakly, her heart thunking.

He put his forehead to hers. "Charlotte, you have to know by now how I feel about you."

She caught her breath, heart pounding, and whispered, "The same way I feel about you, I imagine."

Smiling, he laid his nose alongside hers and nuzzled. "If you promise to pray about us, then I know you'll be thinking about us."

"You didn't even have to ask," she told him, slipping her arms around his neck and laying her cheek against his chest, "but I'm glad you did."

He hugged her close. Then they turned together and walked to his car. She felt pleased and apprehensive at the same time. Oh, how could this possibly work? Nothing had changed, nothing.

"I'll be back late on Wednesday," he told her, "so don't rent out my room."

"I wouldn't give up a sure deal," she teased.

He'd insisted on paying the room rent for this weekend even though no one had expected it. She had no doubt that he'd insist on paying again over Thanksgiving. Tyler Aldrich was a better man, she suspected, than he knew.

Again, she wondered about his spiritual state, dismayed to realize that she'd left it until too late. She'd been so concerned about what seemed to be happening between them that she'd let more important matters slide. Ashamed, she bowed her head.

He placed a kiss in the center of her forehead and got into the car. "See you on Wednesday."

When he turned out onto the highway moments later, she lifted a hand in farewell.

"I'll be waiting," she whispered, and this time she wouldn't let her silly heart obscure what was most important.

Chapter Fourteen

"Frankly, Mother, I never imagined you'd care where I spent Thanksgiving," Tyler said, crossing his legs and adjusting the drape of his slacks over his knee.

He hadn't been surprised when his mother, Amanda, had shown up in his office that afternoon on the day before Thanksgiving. She often came around with some complaint or other. The only surprising thing about it had been the complaint itself, so surprising that he hadn't known quite how to react at first. After a moment, he'd calmly walked her over to the sofa in the seating area of his expansive office and sat down beside her.

"Of course I care!" she exclaimed, but her gaze wandered away from his.

Her pale blue eyes, so like his and Cassandra's, reflected hurt, as they often did, but also something else. Guilt? Dishonesty? He couldn't be sure; he frequently found her difficult to read.

"You never said anything about us getting together for Thanksgiving," he pointed out.

"We're family," she insisted. "Thanksgiving is a family holiday."

"But we've spent many Thanksgivings apart." More, probably, than they'd spent together, although he didn't say so.

Even when he'd been a boy, his parents had been more apt to celebrate the holidays away than at home, often apart from each other as well as their children.

"Well, yes." She lifted her elegant, manicured hands and tilted her neat, platinum head quizzically. "But only when business or important people intervened."

So that was it. She wouldn't mind if the invitation had come from a business associate or someone she considered her social equal, but to her the Jefford family were nobodies.

Tyler sighed. "The Jeffords are very important people to me, Mother."

"That's impossible!" she scoffed, looking away.

Tyler relaxed against the tan suede upholstery and studied her. Slender and petite, her short, pale hair styled fashionably about her tastefully made-up face, Amanda Aldrich looked a good deal younger than her sixty-one years. Then again, she'd had a number of very expensive cosmetic surgeries to make certain of it.

"I assume you've been speaking to Cassandra about this."

Amanda glanced his way and lifted her chin. "She's right, you know. These people are no one."

"If that's so," Tyler said gently, getting to his feet, "then I want to be no one, too." Moving toward the door, he ignored Amanda's gasp. "You'll have to excuse me now. I have an appointment. Have a happy holiday, Mother."

Her face appeared stony when he looked back, but something about it gave him pause. Despite his simmering anger, he reached for kindness "I'm sorry, Mother, but I've already accepted the invitation. We can talk again on Monday, if you like."

"I could understand if it was business," she retorted, folding her arms.

"Yes," he said sadly, "I'm sure you could."

The hour approached nine o'clock on that Wednesday evening before Thanksgiving when Ty parked the sports car in what he'd come to think of as its cubby hole next to what he'd come to think of as *his* room at the Heavenly Arms Motel. Leaving his bag in the trunk, he slipped his hands into his coat pockets and walked across the pavement to the lobby door.

For once, it appeared that his arrival had gone unnoticed, probably because he hadn't stopped beneath the drive-through. This gave him the opportunity to pause for a moment and study those on the other side of the window. Hap, Holt, Grover and Justus sat around the dominoes table, laughing and talking as Justus "shook" the playing tiles by stirring them with his hands. They looked so happy, these people.

Tyler thought of his mother and how *un*happy she'd looked when he'd left her. He wondered if his family had ever been happy. The Jeffords and their friends had all had their share of heartache and grief and little else, yet they had joy.

He'd tasted some of that himself, but only enough to show him how bereft his life really was, and he wanted more. He wanted what the Jeffords and their friends had, and he knew that it started with their faith.

On his last visit Hap had given him a number of Bible verses to read, and Tyler had done so dutifully and repeatedly. He'd even gone out and bought a different translation of the Bible in hopes of better understanding what he read, but he still had questions. He meant to settle this grace thing in his mind before he did anything else.

Going inside, he smiled at the immediate eruption of greeting.

"Ty! 'Bout time you got here."

"Come join us."

"Yeah, Grover's gotta get home," Justus teased. "'Sides, I'd rather have you for a partner. When I lose I can blame it on you." Ty and everyone else laughed at that.

"Charlotte just went into the kitchen," Holt said at the same time that Grover got to his feet.

Ty held up a stalling hand. "Could you hold on a minute, pastor? I've got something on my mind."

"Why, sure." Grover sat down again, and Ty moved around to pull out the chair that Charlotte must have used to observe the game. "How can I help you?"

Ty shrugged out of his tan cashmere coat, draping it haphazardly over the back of the chair before he sat down, placing his hands on the table. "I always thought I was a Christian because I'm a member of a church," he began, noticing the way they exchanged glances around the table, "but I've come to see that it takes more than that. I'm just not sure what."

He saw the way Hap's arm slid across Holt's shoulders, recognizing the satisfaction in the gesture. He realized that these men had been praying for this very thing. They'd known something was lacking in him, and they'd quietly taken the problem to God. He felt a stillness inside himself and a surge of affection.

"Tell you what," Grover said, shifting closer. "What do you say I ask you a few questions? Then you can pray as you feel led. All right?"

"All right."

"Do you believe that Jesus is the Son of God?"

"Yes."

"Do you believe that He lived a sinless life on this earth?"

"I hadn't thought about it, really, but if He's the Son of God, then He must have."

Grover nodded. "And do you realize that He went to the cross blameless, laying down his life to pay the sin price for our sins?"

Tyler gulped. *Our* sins. "My sins, you mean."

He thought of all the angry things he'd said to his brother and sister and parents over the years. He thought of the callousness with which he'd often tended to business and the special treatment he'd expected, so many things he'd done wrong that they suddenly frightened him.

"Yours, mine, everyone's," Hap clarified. "He died for the sins of the whole world."

"Why would He do that?" Tyler wanted to know, understanding suddenly that this one issue lay at the bottom of his confusion.

"Because He loves us," Holt answered. "Think about it. Wouldn't you give up your life for those you love? If they were in danger of eternal peril, wouldn't you say, 'Take me instead'?"

Tyler immediately thought of Charlotte. And Hap and Holt and Ryan, too. Surprisingly, he also thought of Cassandra and Amanda and Preston. Even Justus and Grover and Teddy. When he really thought about it, he knew that he'd take that step for them and others who came to mind. He'd never thought about someone else doing that for him, though.

Gratitude flooded him, and he seemed to have something in his throat, something he couldn't swallow away. "But I don't deserve it," he said.

"That's grace," Hap told him, "giving what isn't deserved."

Suddenly it all came clear.

"Do you know what it means to repent?" Grover asked, and Tyler shook his head. Grover briefly explained, "It means to recognize and turn away from, in other words stop doing, those things that displease God. Once you've made that decision, you need only ask for forgiveness."

"Then you never have to live apart from God again," Justus told him gruffly.

"Doesn't mean you won't mess up," Hap warned, "or have problems."

"Just that you'll be living in the grace of salvation," Grover said.

"And the power of the Holy Spirit," Holt added.

"And just asking begins that?" Ty said.

"Pretty much," Grover assured him. "It is a beginning of sorts, a new beginning."

Ty sucked in a deep breath and bowed his head. A moment later, he felt Hap take his right hand and instinctively offered Justus his left. He stilled his mind, and then he began to pray.

Charlotte gingerly pulled apart the paper bag that she'd just taken from the microwave and dumped the popcorn into a large green plastic bowl. She glanced at the clock, saw that the hour had just gone nine and wondered when Ty would arrive.

The counter behind her fairly groaned with

covered dishes awaiting the food that currently stuffed the refrigerator, including the turkey, which sat ready for the oven. She'd have to be up early in order to get it in on time, but she wouldn't go to bed until Ty had come. She felt too excited to sleep, anyway. Nothing she could tell herself seemed to make any difference, a fact she found somewhat frightening.

She took up the bowl and headed back to the front room, tossing a couple of fluffy pieces of popcorn into her mouth and munching. She stepped through the apartment door, instantly aware of an odd stillness in the front room. For a moment, she saw nothing out of the ordinary. The men sat with their heads bent over the table, but they were not, she came to realize, studying their domino hands. They were holding hands.

She heard a familiar voice say, "Forgive me for all that. I'll do better with Your help."

Ty!

"And thank You for going to the cross for me," he went on. "Thank You for loving me. I never want to live apart from You again, Lord."

The bowl slipped away and hit the floor, no doubt because she'd covered her mouth with both hands to prevent herself from crying out and disturbing the prayer. She didn't hear another word that he said, but after a few moments, everyone lifted their heads and looked at her.

Tyler calmly swiveled on the hard seat of his

chair, got up and came to her, a tender smile on his face. He cupped her cheek in one hand, then went down on his haunches and started sweeping up popcorn. She looked to the others in the room. Grover beamed ear-to-ear, while tears stood in Hap's eyes.

She burbled laughter and dropped down to her knees to help Ty gather up the spilled popcorn. "Sorry," she told the others. "I'll make some more."

Someone replied, several someones perhaps, but the sounds didn't register as words. With the popcorn back in the bowl, they pushed up to their feet. Holding the bowl by the brim with one hand, Ty reached for her hand with the other and led her back into the apartment and toward the kitchen.

"I didn't know you were here," she said quietly, sniffing.

"I only arrived a few minutes ago."

"It doesn't take long," she told him, "to give your heart to Jesus."

He chuckled at that. "Oh, I don't know. It took me weeks. Years, really, when you think about it."

She laughed giddily, and he squeezed her hand.

When they reached the kitchen, she dumped the popcorn in the trash. He lifted a dish towel and peeked beneath it at the cherry and pecan pies she'd baked that day. The aroma of freshly prepared dressing still filled the air. Pressing a hand to his flat stomach, Ty smiled.

"Smells wonderful, especially since I skipped dinner to get here sooner."

Delight shimmered through Charlotte. Quickly she turned toward the refrigerator. She would not taint this pure moment of joy by wishing for more than she knew was possible. "Let me fix something."

"No, you don't have to do that. Won't hurt me to go without, the night before the feast."

"A sandwich, at least," she insisted, taking the makings from the refrigerator.

He relented. "That would be great, thank you."

She slapped together the sandwich, all the time silently rejoicing for the prayer she had overheard. When she finished, she carried the plate to the dining table. He sat, and she hurried back to the kitchen to pour a glass of unsweetened iced tea. When she returned, she found him once more with his head bowed, but he looked up quickly, smiled and picked up the sandwich.

"Won't you sit with me?"

She pulled out a chair and watched him bite into the sandwich. "I know you're used to much finer fare," she began, but he reached out a hand and grasped her wrist, bringing her words and thoughts to an abrupt halt.

"Charlotte," he said, after swallowing, "some of the finest meals I've ever eaten have been right here at this table. Besides, I'd rather sit here eating a bologna sandwich with you than filets mignons with anyone else."

She looked down, warmth spreading through her. "That's a very sweet thing to say."

"Just the truth."

Blinking back tears, she let him eat in peace for a few minutes while she searched her heart. She'd been telling herself that God could not mean Tyler for her, and one of the facts upon which she'd based that conclusion had to do with his spiritual ambiguity. She just couldn't be sure that Ty truly shared her beliefs.

During these past few days, she'd prayed and prayed, as Ty had asked her to. Over and over again, she'd asked God to show her His will and she'd listed the reasons why she and Tyler could not have a future. Now she just didn't know what to think.

She couldn't deny that she cared for Tyler more than she'd ever expected to or that she missed him deeply when he was not with her. Still, they lived in different worlds. Didn't they?

Or did she just not want to leave her own personal comfort zone? If so, what did that say about her faith?

But no, she had to consider her family and their needs.

Shifting to the edge of her seat, she asked, "Can we talk about what just happened in there?"

His lips curled upward. "I'd be delighted to."

They talked for a long while.

"I really thought that joining a church was the same thing as being a Christian," he said at one point, "but after I got to know you and your family, I realized I'd missed something."

Charlotte had no doubt that Tyler had wholeheart-edly turned his life and heart over to Jesus now, and her joy at that knew no bounds, but then he said something that deflated her a bit.

"I can't wait to get back to Dallas and talk to my pastor now. I guess I wasn't comfortable going to him with this because I just didn't know what to ask him. Besides, he knows all of my family and many of our friends, and I guess that was part of it, too. I have to say that he's been pretty glad to see me hanging around the church lately. He's even spoken to me about serving on a committee with one of the church ministries."

Charlotte smiled, but inwardly she sighed. How could they possibly have a future together if he was meant to serve God in Dallas, and she was meant to be here for her family? When she thought about being with him, making a life with him, she knew she wanted that. But fitting into his world seemed… impossible…frightening, even.

She shook off the troubling thoughts and bright-ened her smile, determined to enjoy having him here. Thanksgiving seemed special this year be-cause of Ty, and she wanted to concentrate on her many blessings, beginning with Tyler's growing faith. Everything else came second to that.

"So tell me," she said, changing the subject, "do you have any Thanksgiving favorites?"

He thought about it. "Hmm. Pumpkin pie, of course."

"Got it."

"Cranberry sauce?"

"Homemade by my grandma's recipe."

"Can't wait to dig into that."

"Anything else?"

"Well, football."

Charlotte laughed. "You came to the right place, then."

He carefully wiped away a spot of mustard on his pinky finger before looking at her. "That's not what makes this the right place, Charlotte."

"No?"

Slowly he shook his head side to side. "Seems to me that anyplace you are is the right place." She ducked her head. "I thought about it all the way up here," he went on gently. "I've been thinking about it ever since my mother showed up at my office this afternoon to ask me not to come."

Charlotte jerked her head up, her brow wrinkled. "She asked you not to come?"

He nodded pensively. "We haven't spent all that many Thanksgivings together," he revealed, "and at first I thought her protests were just snobbery, frankly, but the more I think about it, the more I wonder if she's not frightened by the changes in me."

"Changes?"

He slid her a wry look. "Don't pretend I haven't changed since we met."

She thought about the stiff, all-too-charming

stranger who had walked in there that first night and compared him to the friend sitting at ease at her table now. His entire countenance had cleared. Gone were the worries and cares that seemed to have burdened him before. She never wondered if he might be looking down his nose at her, never worried that he might mean ill for her friends or community. Her only fear was that she had come to care too much for him.

"I've changed, too," she admitted. "I thought I had all the answers once, and now…I just don't know anymore what God's will for my life is."

Nodding, Ty braced his forearms on the table. "We'll figure it out together."

Together, she thought, was the problem, but she nodded anyway. What else could she do?

Father in heaven, help me, she prayed silently. *I don't want to hurt this man, and I don't want to go against Your will. Thank You for bringing Ty to Your throne. Thank You for letting us make a difference in his life for You. Just help me figure out where to go from here. I don't want to love him if that's not Your will. I'm so confused. Help me do the right thing, even if that's giving him up.*

But what if that meant leaving here to go with him?

Obviously she still had some serious praying to do.

Could God really mean for her to leave Eden? Could Ty possibly be happy here?

She wanted to believe, wanted desperately to convince herself that God had brought Ty here for more reasons than his spiritual need.

As if that wasn't enough.

Chapter Fifteen

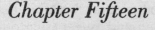

"Well, now, this just might ruin my whole day," Holt drawled, using his fork to pick something out of the hearty serving of dressing on his plate.

"What's that?" Charlotte asked, peering across the heavily laden table.

Holt held up a greenish-brown lump, slid a look at his sister and with a perfectly straight face said, "This piece of celery is at least three centimeters thicker than all the rest."

"Oh, you!" Charlotte picked up a green pea and threw it at him. Uproarious laughter filled the room to bursting.

Holt forked up a huge bite of the dressing and grinned over it at his sister. "Honestly, sis, this meal is as near perfect as it could possibly be."

Everyone agreed, including Ty. The table literally sagged beneath the weight of the feast she had laid before them. In fact, Tyler saw something he'd missed every time he stopped eating long enough to look around the table.

It was enough to make a man abandon healthy eating habits entirely, which is exactly what Tyler and everyone else did for the day, the most thankful day of the year. And, oh, how much they all had to be thankful for!

They'd stood around the table before the meal, four grown men and sweet Charlotte, linked their hands together and took turns praying aloud, praising and thanking the Lord for their many blessings. The festive, jubilant mood still infused them all, especially Tyler. He'd sat himself down and partook with all the enthusiasm of the Jefford men, teasing and laughing and groaning with pure delight.

Tyler couldn't have been happier or more at his ease. He felt, ironically, that he belonged here with these people, and for the first time he asked himself why he couldn't just stay here with them, with Charlotte.

Simply watching her interact with her family gave him great pleasure. Having her smile directed at him from time to time felt almost unbearably sweet.

Yes, he thought, *this is where I want to be. Let the company and my family take care of themselves.*

A pang of guilt surprised him. What would happen to all the people who depended on Aldrich & Associates for their livelihoods if he left the company to the care of his eternally bickering siblings? What would become of them, for that matter? How could his family ever hope to find what he had if he did not lead them to it, and how could he do that if he was not there?

The prayer that he had repeated so often whispered through his mind then.

Lord God, make me a man You are proud to call Your own.

Would such a man abandon the company that he had been charged to lead? Would he abandon his own family?

Tyler listened to the good-natured banter between brothers and sister and heard the unspoken affection and respect that they shared. These Jeffords valued family. Should he do any less?

Perhaps he wished to walk away from the Aldrich family, just put the fussing and backbiting behind him, but would that be right? Did he really even want that?

In all truth, what he wanted most was to feel the same tug of unquestioning love with his brother, sister and mother that Charlotte shared with her brothers and grandfather. Would leaving Dallas and the company achieve that? It didn't seem likely, but he no longer saw a way to live his life apart from Charlotte.

This day did not deserve such heavy thoughts, he decided, and he managed to push them aside. For the most part. He couldn't help wondering from time to time just how his mother, brother and sister were spending the day. They would not, he knew, be enjoying themselves as much as he was, and that saddened him.

No one could maintain a woeful mood in this company on this day, however. Eventually, even Holt, who seemed to have two hollow legs, called a halt. Pushing back his chair, he waved a hand in a sharp sideways movement.

"Enough," he declared.

"More'n enough, if you ask me," Hap corrected.

"More than enough," Holt agreed, rubbing his distended middle. "An embarrassment of riches, in fact."

"Well, then," Ryan proposed, clapping his hands together, "let's get this table cleared so we can get back to football."

"Oh, no," Charlotte protested. "Y'all go on. I'll take care of this."

"No, no, no," Holt insisted. "You cooked. We'll clean."

"Not necessary," she argued, getting up to begin gathering plates.

Tyler quickly rose and plucked up his own, holding it out of her reach. "I'll help her," he told the others.

Holt paused in the process of pushing his chair under the table. Ryan divided a look between Holt and their grandfather. All three of them turned near identical grins on Tyler and Charlotte.

"This is getting to be a habit, Ty," Holt drawled.

"Good habit," Hap inserted.

Ryan sent them both slightly censorious glances before stating firmly, "We'll all clear. If you two would rather wash and dry instead of watching the game, that's up to you. Otherwise, we'll all pitch in later. Well, me and Holt, anyway."

"That's right," Hap said merrily, limping and hitching his way toward the front room. "Got to be some compensation for getting old." Everyone chuckled. "I'll have the TV all warmed up by the time you boys get there. 'Sides, there ain't room enough for all these bodies in the kitchen."

The Jefford brothers shook their heads, grabbing up bowls and platters. Charlotte had sense enough to put down the soiled plates and hurry ahead of them to the kitchen, where she began getting out the necessary storage dishes for the leftovers. Tyler did his bit by gathering up the dirty plates and flatware and ferrying them to the kitchen counter.

In a surprisingly short time, the many leftovers had been safely stowed and the dishes stacked. Charlotte shooed her brothers toward the lobby, then turned to Tyler.

"You, too. I can take care of this."

"No, ma'am. If you're cleaning up, then I'm helping out, and nothing you can say will change my mind."

She looked at the stack of dishes regretfully, sighed and started to follow her brothers. Tyler stopped her with a hand on her forearm.

"I'd rather be right here up to my elbows in dishwater with you than out there with them, much as they tickle me."

She smiled, one corner of her mouth kicking up higher than the other. "What about the game?"

"They can play without me for once."

She relaxed back against the door frame. "Would you be there, actually at that game, if you weren't here?"

"Most likely."

"Why, then?" she asked softly.

"Why am I here instead of there? Or why did I come back at all?"

"Both."

He slid a finger down her cheek. "I had questions, and I knew I could find the answers here." Using his fingertips, he gently pushed her braid off her shoulder. "And then there's the sheer pleasure of your company."

An explosion of hoots erupted from the front room, evoking a smile and a glance in that direction.

"And theirs."

He gazed once again into her complex hazel eyes, noting appreciatively the bits of gold, silvery-blue and soft green. "But it's mostly you, Charlotte," he admitted in a husky voice. "You're why I'm here. And why I'll keep coming back."

She said nothing to that, but he saw a kind of fearful longing on her face that he knew only too well. He'd seen it in his mirror often enough these past weeks.

"Let's do some dishes," he said heartily, turning toward the sink and rolling up his sleeves. "I'll even wash if you want. In fact, I insist on it. I wouldn't know where half this stuff goes, anyway."

Charlotte laughed and reached around him to start the water. Tyler fought the urge to slip his arms around her and pull her close. It struck him then that just being with her like this, even though she was the sweetest thing he'd ever known, would never be enough. Stepping back, he watched her put in the stopper and squeeze in the liquid soap.

Make me a man You are proud to call Your own, he prayed. *I know that will be a whole lot easier if I can have Charlotte in my life, not just once in a while but all the time. I know there are problems with that, but please help me make that happen.*

Ty seemed wound as tightly as an eight-day clock from the moment he walked into the apartment that next morning. Grinning ear-to-ear, he could barely seem to stand still.

"All that food yesterday must've revved your engine," Hap noted over his second cup of coffee.

Tyler bobbed his head in agreement. "Yes, sir. I'm feeling pretty peppy."

He proved that statement by helping Charlotte with her chores. Even after that, however, he seemed bursting with such energy that he rushed her through lunch, saying repeatedly that he needed a good, long walk. Hap laughingly bullied the two of them into coats and sent them off.

Ty fairly danced across the pavement toward the

park, skipping backward much of the time. His exuberance tickled Charlotte. He seemed so happy, and she chalked it up to his growing faith.

"Have you noticed how much of our relationship seems to revolve around food?" he asked at one point.

Our relationship. "What does that mean, I wonder?"

"It means that you're a very good cook, generous to a fault, welcoming, kind—"

"It means that there aren't very many places around here where you can get a decent meal," she interrupted with a chortle.

Empty tree branches clacked together on either side of the street, moved by a swirling breeze that held a damp, cold edge. The gray sky offered no cloud to threaten rain, however, and aside from the wind, the temperature remained lodged in the pleasant range.

"Okay, there is that," he allowed, "but that doesn't mean the rest isn't true, too. You are an excellent cook. Your generosity and kindness amazes me, and no one has ever made me feel more welcome. You, your family…" He looked around, waving an arm in an expansive gesture. "This whole town, really."

Her laughter wafted on the breeze. Why couldn't it stay like this? she wondered. The two of them, always.

And what if "always" is in Dallas?

She shook her head. Late last night she'd decided that she'd been getting way ahead of herself. Ty had asked her to pray about their relationship. He had said that he'd come back to be with her, and now he'd paid her extravagant compliments. That did not mean he would ask her to go to Dallas with him.

True, he'd inquired once before if she would ever consider leaving Eden, but that didn't mean he was making plans for the two of them. She could be agonizing over nothing. Why not just enjoy this time with him and let things play out as God willed?

Turning her face up to the sky, she said, "Have you ever noticed how God gives us glorious moments to get us through the dreary days?"

Tyler considered that for a few moments. "Honestly, the only truly glorious moments I've known have been right here, and I would definitely say those are from God."

She smiled. "You are really on the mountaintop today, aren't you?"

"It would seem so."

They walked on, chatting and laughing about a variety of subjects. Long before they reached the park they could see that the place was deserted. They strolled on, crossing the bridge to the gently rolling ground on the other side. The narrow stream at the bottom of the gully carried leaves with it, little brown and gold boats with crinkled edges.

While weaving their way through the trees, Tyler kicked playfully at the leaves piled in drifts on the ground, a veritable bundle of energy. Suddenly he spun, grasping her lightly by the upper arms.

"I have to get something out of my system."

Staring up at him, she realized that he was seeking permission. "Go on."

To her surprise and delight, he stepped closer. His smile flashed in the instant before he dipped his head and kissed her.

Charlotte felt that kiss all the way to the tips of her toes. Instinctively, she lifted up onto them, her arms drifting about his neck. At length, he lifted his head and sighed.

Charlotte came back to the earth with a thud. She remembered the last time this had happened and that he hadn't seemed inclined to repeat the experience.

"Well, that was less than helpful," he muttered. Charlotte ducked her head, heat staining her cheeks. "Now I just want more."

Her gaze zipped up at that. "Tyler!"

"I know you're not the sort of woman to go around kissing every man she meets," he said, eyes glowing. "I also know that an innocent kiss is all you'd give any man, no matter how you felt about him."

"Except a husband," she blurted, face blazing.

"Since I heartily agree with that sentiment," Tyler said, his voice growing more solemn with every syllable, "I suspect there's just one thing for us to do."

She looked up. Was this the end for them, then, or the beginning? She feared the end, had tried to prepare for it, but something told her that he meant this to be a beginning for them, and she truly did not know what she would do about that. Cautiously, she tilted her head.

"What do you think we should do?" she asked.

"Get married."

Gasping, Charlotte stepped back with one foot. The other remained firmly fixed in place, which pretty well demonstrated how torn she felt. Half of her wanted to throw her arms around him and cry out, "Yes!" The other already grieved what she worried could never be hers.

"B-but how can we? You live in Dallas, and I live here."

"Logistics..." he began, but she cut him off.

"It's more than that! You know it is. We might as well live in different worlds! I don't know anything about society or fashion or suites at the football stadium!"

"Look," he said, stepping closer. "I don't know how it's all going to work out. I only know that I love you and my life will never be complete without you."

Something inside her melted, and one pertinent fact stood out among all the others. She'd fought against it, but she couldn't deny the truth any longer, not to herself, at least. "Oh, Ty."

He took her hands in his and went down on one

knee, saying, "Might as well do this properly." Tears filled her eyes as he formally asked, "Charlotte, will you marry me?"

A sob slipped out of her. She hunched her shoulders as if she could call it back.

"Before you answer," he went on somberly, "you should know that the only way I'll live my life without you is if you convince me that you don't love me, too. Can you do that, Charlotte?"

She shook her head.

"Then I think you'd better agree to marry me, don't you?"

Staring down into his glowing, sky-blue eyes, she could not do anything else. Perhaps it had been only weeks since he'd walked into her life, but from the first moment she had known that God had brought him there.

She knew, too, that her love for him was stronger than her fears about leaving her family and fitting into his, fears that she'd insisted on interpreting as God's will. Even now she didn't know how this would turn out, but she knew that God would take care of it, one way or another, if she just had the courage to take what He offered her now.

Burbling with both tears and laughter, she managed to get out, "Yes, I do."

Tyler came instantly to his feet and drew her into his arms. "Thank You, God. Thank you. We'll work it all out, sweetheart, you'll see. I've been thinking that maybe I should move here."

Stunned, she drew back far enough to gaze up into his face. "But how would that work? What would you do?"

"Do?"

"To earn a living. You have to earn a living."

He lifted both shoulders, mouth flattening into a straight line. "Actually, sweetheart, I don't. Not really. I mean, money is something we'll never have to worry about."

"But can you be happy doing nothing?"

"I'm sure I'll find something to get into."

"What about your family's company?"

He sighed. "I don't know. That's troubling, frankly, but all I can do at this point is pray about it and wait for God to work it all out."

"You're right," she agreed, nodding decisively. "We should pray about it, starting right now."

Smiling, he squeezed her hands before looking around them. "There's the bench over there. Let's sit first."

They turned in that direction, arm in arm. A peacefulness seemed to settle around them, a rightness. Laying her head against his shoulder, Charlotte felt her fears recede and wonder steal in. She couldn't believe what had just happened. She had just agreed to marry Tyler Aldrich!

"I apologize for not being prepared," he told her.

She lifted her head to look at him in confusion. "What do you mean?"

He tapped the tip of her nose with his forefinger.

"I've known since before I left here the first time that I'm in love with you, but I did not expect to ask you to marry me like this."

She squeezed his arm, admitting, "You broke my heart when you went away and I thought I'd never see you again." He covered her hand with his. "I thought that was the end of it."

"I didn't expect to return," he admitted, "but I couldn't stay away, and the more I thought about the two of us being together, the more I dreamed about it, prayed about it, the more right it seemed." His fingers stroked hers. "If I'd been prepared, though, I'd have a ring for you."

"Oh, that." She shrugged because she hadn't even thought about a ring. They had time for rings later. Right now they had other problems, but God would take care of those. If He meant them to be together, and He must, then everything would work out.

"Yes, that," Ty said. "As far as I'm concerned it's the next order of business."

She beamed at him. "Prayer first, ring second. Seems about right to me."

They reached the bench. He pressed a brief kiss to her lips before they sat down. Leaning forward, their elbows braced upon their knees, they clasped hands and bowed heads. Tyler spoke without prompting.

"Thank You, Father. Thank You for bringing me here to this woman. Thank You for making her love me. You've blessed me in so many ways, but this…"

He seemed unable to go on at that point. Heart swelling, Charlotte picked up where he'd left off, saying, "We're stepping out on faith here, Lord. Whatever You have in store for us, we'll face it together, trusting You to show us the way."

Ty spoke again, going on at length in a soft voice about his concerns for his family and their company. "You know I care about them, Lord, but Charlotte is my destiny. I see that now. I just want for my family what Charlotte's has. Help them see that."

Charlotte loved him all the more for his distress on their behalf, and she realized again how much the discord between him and his siblings and mother hurt him. She resolved silently to aid him in rebuilding those relationships. Family, after all, meant so much to her, and, daunting as the idea seemed, they would be her family, too.

They whispered together, "Amen."

Afterward, they lifted their heads to smile and kiss and finally to rise as one.

"Let's go tell Granddad," she said, suddenly giddy with elation.

Tyler laughed and slung an arm about her shoulders. "I confess, I don't think he'll be shocked."

"Or unhappy."

They went as quickly as they could, all but running. Arm in arm, they bumped and bounced and laughed and talked, brimming with joy and hope and love.

"I wonder if Holt could use a partner?" Tyler

mused as they passed the oil pump behind the motel.

She glanced at him in surprise, saw the teasing glint in his eyes and shook her head. They both laughed. The oil field was not for him, at least not the filthy labor part.

"Something will turn up," she predicted gaily.

They rounded the end of the motel wing and crossed the grass to the pavement. Tyler's steps stuttered. Following his line of sight to the drive-through, she saw an expensive foreign luxury sedan parked there.

"Looks like something already has," he announced, suddenly solemn. "That's my sister's car."

Charlotte felt the bottom drop out of her stomach.

Chapter Sixteen

Tyler knew the moment he stepped into the front room that something serious had happened. When he'd seen her car there, he'd expected this to be nothing more than one of Cassandra's famous scenes, the sort she cooked up when she had nothing better to do than make his life miserable. One look at her told him otherwise.

His normally neat, perfectly coifed sister appeared unkempt, or as unkempt as he had ever seen her. Her shoulder-length hair actually looked rumpled, and the dark band that held it back from her face rested at an odd angle on her head. She needed to reapply her lipstick, and, even more alarming, a couple inches of the hem of her long, tailored, dark brown dress hung down. A matching thread trailed from the buckle of one flat shoe.

She'd come to her feet the moment that he and Charlotte had entered through the apartment door and now stood twisting her hands in an uncharacteristic show of concern. Still struggling to his own feet, Hap sent Tyler an apologetic glance.

"What's happened?" he asked.

Cassandra came forward, the lack of a pose indicative of her distress as she exclaimed, "Everything's a mess!"

"Describe 'everything.' No, wait. Describe the mess."

"For starters, we're facing a hostile takeover!"

"You're telling me that the company is being threatened by a hostile takeover?"

"Yes! And you have to stop it!"

Mind whirling, Tyler tried to make sense of this. As a privately owned company, Aldrich & Associates Grocery could only be taken over by an outside entity if one or more of the owners had yielded sufficient shares. He latched onto the first idea that made any sense.

"Spencer-Hatten."

"What? No!"

"You made some sort of deal with Spencer-Hatten, and it's backfiring on you," he accused.

"I didn't!" she insisted, her voice rising to a shriek. "I wouldn't!" For the first time in Tyler's memory, his cool, cryptic sister dissolved into tears. "I wouldn't," she insisted in a small voice.

Stunned, Tyler moved forward to place a hand on her shoulder. "Easy now," he urged gently. He waited until she sniffed and knuckled the tears from her eyes. "So tell me what this is about."

"Shasta," she answered succinctly.

Trust Shasta to make a nuisance of herself at holiday time. Ty sighed, thoroughly ashamed of himself. "I'm sorry I accused you."

Cassandra rolled a gaze up at him. "You had good reason."

He squeezed her shoulder, touched that she would admit such a thing. "What has our step-mother done now?"

"She's married Wilkerson Bishop."

Tyler needed a moment to get his mouth closed. "Wilkerson's eighty-four years old!"

"And our largest shareholder outside the family," Cassandra pointed out needlessly.

The implications were not lost on Tyler. "They still don't comprise a majority."

"They will if they get their hands on Ivory's share."

Frank Ivory had retired as the company's chief financial officer some two years earlier. Then, right before their father had revealed his cancer, he'd stripped Ivory of his seat on the board and awarded it to Shasta.

"Why would Ivory sell his shares to Shasta?"

"Apparently he's still upset about losing his seat, and Wilkerson is offering twice what the shares are worth."

Tyler put his hands to his head, stunned.

"That's not all," Cassandra went on, ducking her head.

Tyler steeled himself. "What else?"

"Mother's in the hospital."

Charlotte gasped, and Tyler's eyebrows shot almost to his hairline. "Why didn't you say so to begin with!"

Charlotte, God love her, stepped up and slid an arm about his waist, placing the other hand in the hollow of his shoulder in a show of support. Without even thinking about it, he reached up and hooked an arm around her shoulders.

Cassandra's chin began to wobble again. "It's all my fault."

"Your fault, how? Shasta's the one who—"

"Mother doesn't even know about that."

"Then what…" He shook his head, at a loss.

"It was something I said," Cassandra admitted. "She was going on and on about how we were losing you, and… It's just such a mess! She started crying yesterday and wouldn't stop. Preston finally called her psychiatrist, and he admitted her."

Tyler pinched his nose. "Great." This was all he needed, one of his mother's well-rehearsed nervous breakdowns.

"Then today when I heard about Shasta," Cassandra went on in a thin voice, "all I could think was that you have to come home!"

Tyler shook his head, feeling torn. He wouldn't have hesitated under other circumstances. He was still the CEO of Aldrich & Associates Grocery, after all, and it had been a long while since his mother had pulled one of these stunts, but now he had Charlotte to consider. Glancing at her, he saw the worried expression on her face and made his decision.

"I'm sorry, but I can't go back now. Charlotte and I have just decided to get married."

"Glory be!" Hap erupted, throwing up his hands.

"My place is here now," Tyler finished firmly.

Cassandra astonished him by again bursting into tears. Shaking her head miserably, she wilted back onto the sofa and covered her face with her hands.

Tyler tensed, momentarily at a loss. Half of him wanted to comfort his sister; half of him expected her to come up snarling. After a moment Charlotte gave him an insistent little nudge. Bowing to her superior knowledge in such matters, he eased himself down and perched on the edge of the sofa next to Cassandra.

"It's all right, Cass," he said, looping an arm around her. "You know how Mother is."

"I've never seen her like this," Cassandra said, dropping her hands and sniffing. "We had words, it's true. Nothing unusual about that, I know. But I said something I shouldn't have and she hasn't been the same since." Cassandra looked up tearfully, whispering, "I'd never have said it if I'd known how much it would hurt her."

Tyler tightened his embrace a bit, saying gently, "She'll get over it."

Cassandra shook her head, mopping at her face with her hands. "I don't think so, not if you abandon us." Suddenly she grasped his hand. "We need you! Mother needs you. The company needs you. We'll never be able to convince Ivory not to sell."

"Just offer him another seat on the board," Tyler suggested. "My sense is that's all he really wants. He can have my seat, actually. You won't even have to create a new one."

"And then what?" Cassandra demanded. "You're the voice of reason on that board. We're all lost without you! You have to come home. Now!"

He'd never thought to hear this. It warmed something inside him to know that his sister actually thought the family and company needed him, but he could not allow himself to be drawn back to Dallas now. Tyler knew what he had to do, and he had every faith God would work it all out for the best. Somehow.

"Cass, I'm sorry, but—"

"No," Charlotte interrupted, stepping forward. Hap made a sound like air leaking from a tire.

Tyler looked up. "Don't worry, honey," he told her, feeling a serenity, a sureness that would undoubtedly center his life from now on. "It's all right." And it was.

Even now, when God seemed to be answering his prayers concerning his family, Tyler understood that he and Charlotte could no longer be separated. They were one heart, joined by the generous will of a loving God, and whatever must be done, they would do together.

From now on Tyler would always try to deal with others, including his own family—especially his own family—with the same gentle, loving acceptance that the Jeffords had demonstrated to him, but without Charlotte by his side, he could only make half an effort at best. Together they would help his family to see that they needed God more than him or anyone, or anything, else.

He reached out a hand to this woman who made him more than he could be alone, this one woman in the whole world who not only completed him but who was undoubtedly God's will for his life.

"I know what I have to do," he said.

"Do you?" Charlotte asked, kneeling at Ty's feet. She exchanged a glance with Hap then looked into Tyler's eyes and saw love unlike anything she had ever dreamed of there. What a good man, not perfect by any means, but wholly surrendered to God, willing to do all that might be asked of him, no matter the personal cost.

How long had he worked and waited, yearning for the kind of acceptance his sister now offered him? How much responsibility had he shouldered, how many solutions had he found, how much regret and grief had he endured for this moment? She could not allow him to abandon that battle.

"We prayed about this not twenty minutes ago," she reminded him gently.

"I know, sweetheart, but I don't want you to think that my word means nothing. I said I'd stay, and I will."

"But is that what God wants, Ty? Don't you see? You told God how much you love your family and how you want them to have what you've found in Him, and this is His answer."

Tyler cupped her face in his hands and said exactly what she expected him to say. "Darling, you're my family now, even if we're not married yet. And you will always comes first with me."

"Yes, of course," she said, smiling through the tears that gathered in her eyes. She didn't know if she could do this. She only knew that she had to try, for Tyler's sake. She wouldn't think of how much she would miss Eden and her family, only of how much she loved him. *Oh, Father, help me,* she prayed silently. *Help me do this for Ty.* "And from this day forward you will always come first with me," she vowed, "but your place is in Dallas."

"I won't go," he insisted, shaking his head. "Not without you."

Charlotte took a deep breath, her heart beating a wild tattoo. "Then I'll just have to go with you."

Tyler seized her by the upper arms. "Charlotte, you don't mean that."

"I think I must mean it," she said, smiling and weeping at the same time.

"You see it's like this, son," Hap rasped. "God's got purpose for you in Dallas. Your family and your company need you, and if Charlotte belongs with you, then that's where both of you got to go."

Holt and Ryan walked into the room just then. Holt held a fork poised over a plate of pecan pie. "Both of who?"

Hap hitched around. "Ty and Charlotte's getting married."

Ryan pumped an arm in a whoop of approval. "Yes-s-s!"

"Who's this, then?" Holt asked, stepping forward to beetle his brow at Cassandra.

"Oh, this here is Ty's sister, Cassie," Hap said. Cassandra said nothing about the nickname. "She's a mite upset," Hap went on. "Their mom's in the hospital and some other stuff." Hap swirled a hand as if to say it was all too confusing for him.

"I'm sorry to hear that," Ryan immediately remarked.

Holt stared at his sister, and she knew his thoughts immediately. She pushed up to her feet and went to her brother.

"It isn't just that I love him," she said softly. "I love him enough to go where he has to go."

Holt's lips flattened, but then he cut off a big bite of the pie and gulped it down. "Ryan and me—" he grumbled, wiping a corner of his mouth with the pad of his thumb "—we figured this was coming."

"We have a plan," Ryan announced, grinning ear-to-ear.

"A plan?" Charlotte repeated.

"To take care of stuff around here," Ryan said, as Holt studiously forked in another huge bite of pie. "We've got it all figured out. We'll both pitch in. With some part-time help, we'll be fine."

"We can afford full-time if we need to," Hap mused, "especially if we throw in room and board."

Holt looked at what was left of his pie, a rueful twist to his lips. "Well, room, anyway," he amended with a sigh.

Charlotte wondered with dismay who would cook for them, but she knew they wouldn't starve. They could manage until they could hire someone. Nodding grimly, she swiped at the tears trickling down her face and whispered, "I love you all so much."

"But you belong with Ty," Hap rasped.

Tyler appeared at her side, sliding an arm around her waist. He looked down at her, and she read the troubled expression in his eyes. "Sweetheart, are you sure about this?"

"Yes," she answered. Then, because she could never lie to him, said, "No. What I mean to say is, I'm not sure how it's all going to turn out, but I think we have to do this. I think *I* have to do this." Fear of failing Ty coiled in her belly, but she ignored it, lifting her chin. It was time she stepped out on faith instead of just talking about it.

Tyler's gaze held more than a little worry, but he nodded, obviously relieved. She took joy in that.

"You better get moving," Holt told her, "before

I decide I can't live without your pie." The quip fell flat.

She couldn't believe she was doing this, but she bullied aside her doubts and threw her arms around Holt. He held out the pie to protect it and pecked a kiss on her temple, but his tight smile didn't fool her. She knew he held back his tears with Herculean effort.

She went to Ryan next. "I hope you two know what you're letting yourself in for."

Ryan winked at Ty, teasing, "Anyone can make a few beds."

All her doubts rushed over her in that moment. "As if! It's not just making beds, it's—"

"I expect I know a thing or two about what it takes to keep this place running," Hap interrupted. "If three grown men can't do it, well, God'll provide."

"I know He will," Charlotte agreed, moving toward her grandfather with a heavy heart.

What a blessing he had been to her! Once she had thought her grandfather would forever be the center of her world. She had believed that anything that took her from there and him could not be right, but that was before Ty.

Oh, Father, don't let this be a mistake. Surely it shouldn't be this difficult!

"Granddad," she began, her chin trembling. He cut her off, engulfing her in a bear hug.

"I know what you're gonna say, sweet girl, but I never expected you to give up your life for me. I'm plenty old enough to be on my own. Me and the boys will work it all out. God's got something else for you to do."

"We'll be fine," Ryan said, joining the hug. "We have a plan. You go with Ty and help him out. Sounds like he needs it."

Holt pointed at Tyler then. "Speaking of plans, we're expecting to hear wedding plans as soon as your mom's able."

Tyler shook his head. "You're just going to trust me to take Charlotte off like this?"

The brothers looked at each other. "If we can't trust you to take her now, we sure can't trust you with the rest of her life," Ryan declared.

"Besides," Holt added, "we know our girl. Her we can definitely trust."

Charlotte hugged them both again, whispering, "Thank you."

"You just be happy," Hap instructed, nudging her to get moving. She couldn't think about that now. What if she could never be happy in Ty's world? She only knew that she would no longer be happy in her own world without him.

"Cassandra," Charlotte said, turning to Tyler's sister, her mind awhirl with a hundred concerns, "I'll need you to help me put together a suitable wardrobe as soon as possible. Can you do that?"

Cassandra blinked, looked at Ty, and then she smiled in a happily calculating manner. "I'd be delighted."

"Thank you." But her wardrobe was surely the least of what she faced, Charlotte knew. Whirling, she kissed Hap on his ragged cheek then rushed toward the apartment door, calling over her shoulder to Ty, "I'll throw some things into a bag and meet you outside."

Behind her, she heard Hap chuckle. "You best scoot, son. She's unstoppable once she's got her game plan on."

"Speaking of that," Ryan interjected, "you can expect us in your sky box at the next home game."

The last thing Charlotte heard before the apartment door swung closed behind her was Tyler's laughter. She wished that she could feel as happy and carefree as he sounded, but all she could do was gird herself for the battles ahead. How many, she wondered, before she could lay claim to any real peace in her life again?

Despite the doubts that crowded in on her, however, she clung to the hope of certainty. If the ground beneath her feet suddenly felt unsafe, then she'd just have to trust that angels would watch over her.

Chapter Seventeen

Charlotte felt strongly that Ty needed to see his mother as soon as possible, so they decided to drive straight to the hospital. Cassandra followed in her car. Along the way they spoke prayers for Amanda's well-being and Ty's wisdom in dealing with her. Once they reached the city, he pointed out landmarks relevant to his life, including the towering edifice in the distance, where he owned a penthouse.

"Just another word for a larger-than-average apartment," he commented mildly when Charlotte widened her eyes at the word *penthouse.*

Mentally gulping, Charlotte smiled and said nothing. Inside, she quivered with nerves, her stomach knotting painfully. She truly believed that she and Ty belonged together, but her new role in his life terrified her. The weeks and months ahead were bound to be difficult ones. Only with God's help could she hope even to get through them, but get through them she would. Somehow.

They left the car with a valet at the hospital entrance. At some point Cassandra had fallen well behind them, but Tyler showed no concern.

"She knows her way around. She'll show up later."

He'd informed his sister via cell phone of their intentions, and she'd told him their mother's room number. Clutching his hand, Charlotte allowed him to lead her through the gleaming building to a central desk, where he spoke with a volunteer before being shown to a private elevator tucked into an out-of-the-way corner. They rode swiftly up to the correct floor. When they stepped off, a uniformed security guard nodded at them, and Charlotte's confidence abruptly faltered.

Gulping, she looked down at the jeans and sweater that she wore beneath her usual old quilted jacket. Why hadn't she at least exchanged her athletic shoes for flats? As if reading her mind, Tyler, still clad in his comfortable jeans and a simple shirt himself, dropped a kiss on her forehead.

She tried to put aside her fears and believe that God controlled the situation. Back in Eden, she hadn't doubted this was the right thing. She told herself that her place, now and forever, was at Tyler's side. She just hoped that she didn't embarrass him in any way.

They walked down a broad, shiny corridor that

more closely resembled a plush hotel than any hospital Charlotte had ever seen. At the quietly bustling nurses' station, they were met by a distinguished, middle-aged man in a pristine white lab coat. His relief was clear.

Tyler introduced Dr. Olander, identifying Charlotte as his fiancée. The doctor quickly masked his surprise, but if Charlotte could have crawled into a hole at that moment, she would have.

After issuing congratulations and best wishes, the doctor got down to business. "I've never seen Amanda like this." As he spoke, he led them toward a door with the appropriate number affixed to it. "She's been weeping since she came in, and all she'll say is that she's a complete failure, especially as a mother."

Tyler dropped a perplexed look on Charlotte and pushed open the door. The "room" turned out to be a suite with a private sitting area.

Charlotte looked to Ty. "Maybe I should wait here."

He skimmed a knuckle across her cheek. "I know how hard this is for you, but I need you in there with me. If I thought I could handle this on my own, I'd never have asked you to come."

How could she refuse that? The doctor pushed into the inner room, announcing, "Amanda, Tyler is here."

He stepped aside, revealing a small figure in a high, narrow bed. That figure rolled to face them as

ıey moved forward. Even without makeup, her
ᴠhite-blond hair sticking out at odd angles and
wollen, red-rimmed eyes, she appeared much
ᴏunger than her sixty-one years. One look at Ty,
ıough, and she burst into noisy sobs.

To Charlotte's surprise, he did not immediately
ᴏ to Amanda. Instead he looked rather helplessly
t Charlotte. He seemed even more at a loss with his
ıother than he had with his sister. After a moment,
'harlotte pantomimed a hug. He looked doubtfully
ack to the bed.

Finally, with Charlotte's hand still gripped in
is, he walked forward, saying, "Mother, what is
ıis about?"

Amanda's sobs rose to a wail.

Frowning at him, Charlotte gave him a tiny
ıove, indicating with a nod of her head that he
ıould sit on the bed and moderate his tone. He
ᴏked somewhat desperate at that, but then he
ıngerly perched on the edge of the bed, saying,
t'll be all right. We're here now."

"We?" Amanda queried weakly, sniffing and
ᴏking up.

Ty tugged Charlotte closer, announcing firmly,
Ꭲhis is the woman I'm going to marry. Charlotte,
is is my mother, Amanda."

The shock not only stopped Amanda's tears, it
ᴏunded her eyes and mouth to comic proportions.
ᴏrcing a smile, Charlotte remarked to herself that
least she now knew where Ty got those gorgeous

eyes of his. The bedside manner was something they'd definitely have to work on, though.

"M-married?" Amanda's bleary gaze sought out Charlotte. "You're that Jefford woman, aren't you?"

"That's right," Charlotte answered, hoping her smile looked more cheery than it felt.

"I want you to tell me what brought this on," Ty said.

"First things first, though," Charlotte interjected gently, addressing Amanda. "Ty and I are going to pray for you. Then we'll all talk."

Amanda appeared stunned. Charlotte heard the door close softly behind them as the doctor slipped out. Heart pounding, she moved sideways to place both of her hands on Ty's shoulders and bow her head. Despite the distinct impression that Amanda did not follow suit, Charlotte's heart swelled as Ty began to speak.

"Thank you, Lord, for these two women. You know how much I love them and how much I need them. We all need Your guidance, and right now, my mother needs Your healing. Whatever's wrong, I know You can fix it, and while You're doing that, I ask You to make me a better son and a good husband, a man of whom You can be proud."

When he was done, Amanda lurched upward and threw her arms around her son, sobbing again. Tyler, thankfully, hugged her tightly, whispering, "It's all right. Please don't cry. Everything's going to be fine."

Suddenly, she grasped Charlotte's hand and fell back onto the bed, clutching at Ty. "Oh, son, I'm sorry for being so weak and stupid!"

Ty shook his head, smiling. "Amanda Aldrich may be a lot of things, but weak and stupid are not among them."

"Oh, yes, they are," she insisted. Her grip on Charlotte intensified as she switched her gaze once more to Charlotte's face. "I've been lying here making myself sick because I didn't think my son loved me." Her face crumpled, but she went on. "And why should he? I don't even know how to be a mother. I never have!"

Charlotte's heart lurched inside her chest. She'd been right to come. God was at work here, and He would surely work out everything else. Over time she would come to miss Eden and her family less and less, to love Ty and his family more and more.

"Now, now," Ty crooned, petting his mother's head.

"I'm sorry," she wailed, "but when Cassandra said that you'd told *her* you love her, I—I was so...so...*jealous!*"

"Mother!" Ty gasped, sounding a bit exasperated.

"Then I realized that maybe I'd never told any of my children how much I love them, and I *do*," she squeaked, "I do!"

"Oh, Mom," Tyler said, gathering her close. He lifted a glance at Charlotte, his eyes speaking volumes. Charlotte nodded in acknowledgment. "It's all right," Tyler said, rocking Amanda slightly. "Everything's going to be different now, I promise."

She pushed back a bit then and in a slightly reproving voice said, "You've never called me Mom before." Then she looked up at Charlotte, adding, "I suppose I have you to thank for that, young lady." Lifting her chin, she whispered, "Thank you."

Charlotte laughed with delight. Relief and understanding swept through her. Maybe their lifestyles were as different as night and day, maybe she wasn't a fashion plate or from an influential family, but people were just people, after all, and every one of them needed the same things.

To her joy, she realized that she had more to offer Tyler and his family than she'd realized.

In many ways she'd just been marking time in Eden. Now she and Ty must forge a new world for themselves, for all of them. If she lost something precious in the bargain, well, it would be worth it. Besides, Eden would always be there for them. And they would never have to worry about having a room when they went to visit. With God's help, she could adapt. She must, for what other choice was there?

A palace, Charlotte thought with some dismay, glancing around Ty's sumptuous, elegant penthouse. He'd remarked earlier that *penthouse* simply meant a larger-than-average apartment, but the

entire apartment that she shared with Hap back at
the Heavenly Arms Motel would fit into just the
master suite of this place.

Glass and shiny steel lightened dark, glossy
wood, black lacquer and rich burgundy, making for
an undeniably beautiful decor, yet the place felt
colder and emptier than even the most shabby room
at the motel. She'd have preferred to see a bit of
personal clutter, frankly, but even the enormous
bathroom displayed all the hominess of an operating room.

Looked like she had her work cut out for her. But
she could do this, she reminded herself. With God's
help she would make this place a home.

"You don't like it," Ty said, leading her back to
the living area after they'd settled Amanda into the
guest room across the hall from Charlotte's.

It had been decided that Amanda would stay there
with them after checking out of the hospital, at least
for the time being. Later, Ty had suggested, Charlotte
might be more comfortable the other way around,
but the idea of moving in with his mother, even tem-
porarily, filled Charlotte with gloom, which she
struggled mightily to disguise. Fortunately, Cassandra and Preston had arrived just about then and were
now spending a private moment with their mother.

"It's fabulous!" she insisted, lifting both arms to
encompass the expansive room with its gorgeous
furnishings, ceiling-to-floor windows and
enormous, hidden television screens.

"Look," he said, coming forward to take her into his arms. "I never expected to live here forever. Actually, I always figured I'd wind up in a house in Highland Park, not some little town in Oklahoma. Just goes to show, huh?"

Charlotte blinked. "Do you mean that? You still plan to make our home in Eden?"

He drew back slightly. "Of course. Wouldn't you rather raise our family in Eden than here?"

"Well, yes, but what about your family?"

"I suspect we'll never be the same," Cassandra said, walking into the room, "and maybe that's a good thing." She'd changed into a teal silk pantsuit and twisted her hair up into a wispy, trendy clump.

Preston, Tyler's brother, followed in a somewhat more subdued, thoughtful manner. Charlotte had thought Ty to be the best-dressed man she'd ever seen, but Preston, whose thick, wavy, medium-brown hair seemed a perfect mixture of Cassandra's milky-blond and Ty's dark, chocolate color, might have been a male model. Charlotte wondered if she had ever been that comfortable in her clothes.

She tugged her mind back to matters of more importance. "What about your company?" she asked Ty.

"Please," Preston said, sounding bored as he dropped down into a leather club chair. "This is the twenty-first century."

Tyler tucked Charlotte close to his side and turned to his brother. "Meaning?"

Preston examined his fingernails. "You can run the company from anywhere. All you really need is a good Internet connection. DSL should do it."

Tyler rubbed his chin. "Actually, it would have to be a satellite connection."

Striking a pose, Cassandra shrugged negligently. "So you'll get a satellite link."

Hope rising, Charlotte looked to Ty. "Could we?"

Nodding, he mused, "Probably need a phone, too. The cell coverage leaves a lot to be desired." He looked at her. "It would mean a good deal of travel back and forth, I imagine."

Preston spread his hands. "So keep this place for when you're in town."

"Are you saying that you think I should continue running the company?" Ty asked pointedly.

Preston lifted an insouciant gaze. "Who else?"

"You didn't think you were going to get out of it that easily, did you?" Cassandra said, folding her arms.

Tyler looked between his brother and sister. "The two of you would have to take on more responsibility."

Something played across Preston's lips. "Think you can trust us?"

"Yes," Ty answered firmly.

"The infighting has gotten rather boring of late," Preston said, trying not to look too pleased. Crossing his legs, he dropped his gaze. "I'll do my best."

"I know you will." Ty looked at his sister. "Cassandra?"

She broke into a wide grin. "You know, it's just possible that we could make the best management team ever if we really put our minds to it."

"Amen," Ty agreed delightedly. He gazed down at Charlotte, his blue eyes glowing. "It'll take some time, you understand, to get things reorganized here, and then of course we have to find a piece of property around Eden and design and build our dream house."

"We have our whole lives," she told him, so happy she could burst. What a fool she had been to limit God in any way. All He'd ever required of her was surrender to His will. "But first things first, as you said earlier. We have a wedding to plan, remember?"

Smiling, Ty hugged her tightly. "How could I forget? And just so you know, I have recently discovered that I definitely do not believe in long engagements."

"That makes two of us then."

"Now," Cassandra said in a very businesslike manner, "I suppose the wedding should be in Eden."

Ty and Charlotte looked at each other. "At the First Church," he confirmed.

Charlotte beamed. "Grover will be so pleased."

"Just family and close friends, I'd think," Cassandra mused, "but of course we'll need to have a second reception here."

Tyler opened his mouth, ostensibly to object, but Charlotte elbowed him discreetly, aware that compromise behooved her and would henceforth be a large portion of her life. Besides, she would not pass up an opportunity to befriend her future sister-in-law. Her life, it seemed, had irrevocably changed in amazing ways.

"I trust you and your mother will take care of those details for us," Charlotte told Cassandra.

Tyler made a choking sound that quickly turned into a short cough. Less concerned with politesse, Preston baldly stated, "Try and stop them."

"You can count on us," Cassandra said to Charlotte, ignoring her brothers completely. Turning, she hurried back in the direction from which she'd come, muttering, "I hope Mother is not asleep yet."

Preston rose languidly. "I'm leaving before I get dragooned into helping out." He had just turned away when Tyler stopped him.

"Preston?" The younger man looked back. Tyler stepped forward uncertainly. "I'd like to say something to you, something that should've been said long ago."

Preston smiled slightly. "I love you, too, bro." Then he walked away.

Elated, Charlotte went to slide her arms about Tyler's waist. "Things seem to be turning out better than I ever imagined."

"You can say that again," he told her, lifting his

own arms about her. "I'll take you home tomorrow if you want."

"Hmm." She considered, feeling very much like a cat in cream. "Better wait on that. I think I have some shopping to do."

He laughed. "Buy anything you want. We'll start at the jewelers."

Charlotte sighed. "I'm afraid I could get used to this."

"I certainly hope so. Just like I got used to Eden."

The days passed in a whirlwind. It was more than a week before Charlotte saw her home again. They returned to Eden in a car laden with new purchases, and that did not count what Ty or Cassandra or Amanda had had shipped ahead or what would arrive later.

They'd planned the ceremony for the following Friday, the first Friday in December, and Charlotte had been gratified to find the church elaborately decorated for Christmas. She showed off her ridiculously extravagant ring and hung on to Ty as if he might disappear in a puff of smoke.

On Sunday evening, they took a lingering leave of one another. Ty had to get back to Dallas to tend to business there so he could afford to take time off for the honeymoon. Since she had no passport, they had decided on a very exclusive resort in the mountains of Colorado. Ty had promised her horse-drawn sleigh rides and skiing lessons.

He would return on Thursday with his family, a thought that made Charlotte's stomach cramp when she realized how primitive they were apt to find their accommodations.

She need not have worried. The Aldriches swept into town like traveling royalty and behaved just as graciously. Amanda had the rehearsal dinner and the reception catered, all the way from Dallas, in the church fellowship hall. Cassandra produced a mountain of lush poinsettias, sumptuous gold satin and thousands of twinkling lights, with which her personal decorator built a glorious bridal arch unlike anything Eden had ever seen. Preston's gift to them was a stringed quartet that produced hours of classical music.

The ceremony itself was somewhat unconventional.

Hap escorted Charlotte down the candlelit aisle of the packed church in her gorgeous new wedding gown. Her brothers met her at the altar and gave her hand in marriage, then stood at her side while Cassandra and Preston stood with Tyler.

Grover seemed somewhat overwhelmed, but as Hap would say later, "He got her done."

Charlotte stood with tears in her eyes and joy in heart to repeat her vows to Tyler and then laughed when Ty, the suave and debonair man from Big D, bobbled his own lines.

"Oh, forget it," he exclaimed. "I love you, Charlotte, with my whole heart, you and your family and my family and this whole town. The day I blundered in here was the most fortunate day of my life, and I praise God for it. With His help I'll make you the best husband I possibly can."

"You aren't apt to get a better deal than that," Justus Inman called from behind them.

Everyone laughed, and Grover quickly pronounced them husband and wife. After a long kiss that produced catcalls and more laughter, they ran back up the aisle, then stood arm in arm at the back of the church, watching their families file toward them.

"We're going to be so happy," she whispered.

"Yes, we are," he told her, hugging her close.

They watched Hap offer Amanda his arm, then hobble along beside her with his hitching step somehow matched to her elegant stride.

"All of us."

Laughing, they ran out into the December night, warm despite the chill of the evening, understanding just how richly God could and would bless His obedient children.

It went far, far beyond monetary things, from creation to salvation to the heart's desires.

And to think, Charlotte, said to her husband later, that she'd almost missed out!

Just by opening herself to it, by putting aside her assumptions and being willing to let God have His way, she'd received one of the greatest blessings of all.

True love.

Only that could build a bridge between two worlds.

* * * * *

Will Charlotte's brother Holt
ever find his own true love?
Be sure to pick up
HER SMALL-TOWN HERO,
coming in December 2008,
only from Love Inspired.

Dear Reader,

Welcome to Eden, Oklahoma—God's country, land of oil! I grew up in south central Oklahoma. That's where I gained the foundation upon which my life is built, where I received the Lord and first dreamed of being an author. That's also where I met the love of my life.

I've tried to bring the feel and spirit of the place to you and to impart some of what I learned in the little church that my grandfather helped to build with his own hands. What better place to set a series about love and faith and the goodness of our Heavenly Father? It is, in many ways, a world apart. I hope you'll enjoy your visit there as much as Tyler Aldrich does and that you will be as richly blessed.

God bless,

Arlene James

QUESTIONS FOR DISCUSSION

1. One of the great burdens in Tyler's life was the acrimonious relationship he had with his family, all of whom were fighting for control of the family company and wealth. Is great financial wealth a hindrance to healthy relationships? Why or why not?

2. Tyler had attended church his entire life, mostly for the sake of image. He never understood why he should really be attending church. Is his wealth a hindrance to his spiritual maturity?

3. It is often said that ours is not a God of confusion. Why, then, are committed Christians like Charlotte subject to confusion at times?

4. Until she fell in love with Tyler, Charlotte thought she knew God's will for her life. Yet, Ecclesiastes 3:10–10 speaks to the "seasons" of our earthly lives. In light of this, does God's will for our personal lives ever change? Is this what happened to Charlotte?

5. The Jeffords saw Tyler Aldrich as someone in need. As Christians we are taught to minister to the needy, but how do we define "needy," and is

it possible for the financially wealthy to be as needy as the less affluent?

6. The Jeffords ministered to Tyler in a very personal fashion, but the average Christian does not have the opportunity to mingle with the very wealthy. How can we, as Christians, go about ministering to the needs of the financially wealthy?

7. At one point, during a prayer service, Tyler feels "a presence." Is it possible in this day and age to feel the *physical* presence of God?

8. As Tyler fell deeper and deeper in love, his love for his family began to come to the fore. Is this because he was falling in love with Charlotte?

9. Tyler eventually found peace through surrender to Christ. Given his financial resources, he could have done much for the cause of Christ. Should financially wealthy Christians feel guilty about spending money on themselves or loved ones?

10. As Charlotte fell deeper and deeper in love, she began to question her understanding of God's will for her life. Is this because she had been fooling herself about her commitment to Christ?